THE LITTLE HORSE

THE LITTLE HORSE

THORVALD STEEN

Translated by James Anderson

Seagull
BOOKS
LONDON NEW YORK CALCUTTA

Seagull Books, 2024

First published as *Den lille hesten* by Thorvald Steen

© Forlaget oktober, 2002 ·

First published in English translation by Seagull Books, 2014

English translation © James anderson, 2014

This translation has been published with the financial support of NORLA

ISBN   978 1 8030 9 447 2

British Library Cataloguing-in-Publication Data
a catalogue record for this book is available from the British library Typeset

in by Seagull Books, Calcutta, India
Printed and bound by Hyam Enterprises, Calcutta, India

CONTENTS

THE LITTLE HORSE

Even Reykholt, in the north-west of Iceland, an island in the middle of the Atlantic, was overtaken by war. This is the story of almost anywhere in the world, in any age. The ruins are the scars left by man. Dreaming about one another, and loving and killing one another, are some of humanity's oldest characteristics, and come as easily to it as using words. As the scraping and cleaning of Reykholt's remaining foundations proceeds, it's not just the closeness of antiquity one senses. It's the smell of man.

18 SEPTEMBER
1241

Most people have no idea how many days they have left to live. He believed he had many years before him. What he would say at the moment of reckoning hadn't occupied his mind at all. He dressed himself, combed his hair and drank a ladleful of water from the bucket by his bed. There was no one to be seen outside. He gazed up at the sky, that ancient parchment on which the sun and moon sketch day and night.

Snorre Sturlason had five days left to live.

The thought of Orækja came suddenly, as it always did. Although you've brought up your children, it doesn't mean you understand them. His sole surviving son was a mess of a man. He would rather think of Margrete, who was going to visit him the following day. He imagined her, those intense eyes, that hair, her quick movements, long fingers, the smile, the hips. He wondered what it would be like to kiss that small mouth.

On that same morning, a day's ride away, it was decided that Snorre should die on Saint Maurice's eve. Nobody breathed a word of this to him. He had his enemies, of course, but at that moment he had no inkling that anyone would be prepared to hack him to death on his own estate. The killers made their plans in the knowledge that they had King Håkon's full support.

Snorre opened the door and looked out at Reykholt. The wind was blowing. The light fell softly on him. Morning filled the yard with light. He was incorporated into the day. By the rising ground, just behind the anvil where Torkild fashioned arrowheads, he could see the toolstore. Torkild was a great, broad-shouldered, useful man who was always a boon when anything had to be repaired or adapted. Snorre wanted a word with Torkild. As he crossed the well-trodden turf, he felt his toes being squashed together in his leather shoes.

A little way off, the sheep waded through the golden-brown field spreading out, enveloped in silvery grey light. Sheep, he thought, had the long faces of martyrs. But why had they come so close to the farm?

Snorre walked over to the cart in front of the toolstore. He ran his forefinger over its shaft to see if the dew had left any traces of moisture. He let his finger brush once, twice along the woodwork. What was that sound he could hear? It came from the toolstore. Was Torkild shaping horseshoes on his anvil? Snorre went closer. They weren't hammer blows. But what were they? He gazed out across the gentle contours of the land beyond the estate, across the nearby stream and the river behind it that had its source in the mountains and glaciers on the horizon.

There was always something that needed repair or attention on the large farm. On several occasions, Snorre had begged Torkild to stop work earlier than was his custom. Torkild had smiled and said that Snorre oughtn't to poke fun at him. He continued to work just as feverishly in the evenings and was the last to turn in. And the next morning, it was always Torkild who was up first. The work of the forge was important to his self-esteem, Snorre realized. Torkild was the same age as Snorre, in his early sixties, but much lighter on his feet. Now Snorre wanted to wish him good day and thank him for all he'd done. Then he would ask Torkild if there was anything he wanted.

A little friendliness wouldn't hurt. Snorre nodded and mumbled to himself. Things hadn't been entirely easy between them ever since Snorre had enjoyed Torkild's wife night after night three years ago. She ran away from the estate, and no one had set eyes on her since. Surely Torkild had got over that by now? Occasionally, Torkild had complained that his earnings were too small. Snorre had replied that poverty was a step on the way to happiness in the next life.

Like the modest man he was, Torkild would doubtless reply that he neither needed nor wanted anything. So Snorre would leave a silver coin on the cask inside the door.

Was it the wind that made it impossible to pinpoint where the sound was coming from? The door to the tool-store was shut and bolted. When he walked round to the rear of the store he saw it was the back door that was banging. Snorre grasped the door. 'Torkild!' he shouted.

No one answered. The anvil in front of the door had four straightened nails lying on it. He opened the door wide. The tools were arranged neatly along the walls. Hammers, awls, axes, spokeshaves and saws hung on the side wall in order of size. An upset wooden cup yawned on the cask just within. Snorre entered. The room was empty. The door banged shut behind him, leaving him in inky darkness.

'Torkild,' he said in a low, hesitant tone. He kicked the door open again, lumbered across the yard and called. Nobody answered.

Snorre walked up the slope. His eyes wandered over the plain, searching for sheep in the distance. He glanced at the bare ridge that rose to the north of the estate. His gaze ran over the dry, almost sand-coloured patch of ground beneath the summit. The earth was puckered like old skin after the parching summer, full of cracks and ragged clumps which felt like stones beneath the soles of his shoes. He called Oræja's name and cursed. For an instant, he conjured up Oræja's mother. They'd only been together a few nights. When he'd visited her some months later, she'd put on weight. The last time Snorre had seen Oræja, at the house of his nephew Tumi, the atmosphere between father and son had been congenial, for once. Snorre wiped the sweat from his brow and went back inside, seated himself on the long bench, rested his elbows on the table, folded his hands and stared straight ahead.

To have such a son! What had he done wrong? The worst of it was that he constantly needed this murderer's help. Oræja loved his father. As if that made it any easier.

Were a couple of horses passing outside? No one was due to leave now! Snorre started up, bounded towards the door, pushed it open and just managed to get a glimpse of Torkild's back; he was leaning forward on the horse, his face pressed into its mane, at full gallop. Snorre hobbled after it for a short distance. His calves and ankles had swollen during the past six months, but he didn't know why. Torkild and his young helper, Svein, rode side by side. Snorre shouted. They didn't turn. No one else took up the pursuit. They were riding towards Surtshellir, the long cave. His most trusted man at Reykholt was decamping! He must have persuaded his assistant, a red-haired stripling of a lad, to go with him.

'Traitors!' Snorre yelled after them. 'Thieves! Rabble!' His best smith had deserted with no word of explanation.

Snorre bellowed at Torkild once again before the horses were out of sight. Why hadn't anyone prepared him for this? He stared in disbelief at the cloud of dust they'd left behind. Snorre walked quickly back to the house. He stopped in the doorway. What if someone had heard him shouting?

Snorre's inability to control Orækja was one thing, but to have his own servants treating him in this manner! Could it have been the anticipation of meeting Margrete that had caused him to take his eye off the situation? He glanced at the other houses. He placed the flat of his hand on his forehead, and drew it down over his face, over the hooded eyelids, the prominent nose and the bearded chin. Ought he to call for Kyrre, who oversaw the work on the estate? But if he started going from door to door at Reykholt asking questions, wouldn't they assume he was uneasy?

How many people were on the estate? Kyrre was the one who had the precise tally. He didn't know each one of them himself, but there must have been a good seventy in all. And how many of these were servants? No, he couldn't remember. He couldn't recall the names of everyone who worked at Bessastadir either, or the other farms for that matter. He couldn't be everywhere.

The Reykholt estate, the hub of the old church fief, wasn't especially large but the whole fief was considerable. It was the reason he'd bought the estate in 1206. Neither its appearance nor its situation were particularly grand, but it was well situated. Roads to the west, south and north ran close to the property. It's not easy getting a sense of one's own wealth, but when Snorre gazed at the tarred houses within the enclosing ramparts, his eyes softened with satisfaction. First, he looked at the north gate, then at the south. They were both in good repair. The dwellings stood firm and he could see the sheep and cows grazing peacefully a little way off on the other side of the ramparts. Even though his brother Thordr had called Reykholt the 'forlorn fortress', Snorre took no notice.

It was all his. After Hallveig's death two months earlier, he was the sole proprietor. It was thirty-five years since he'd bought Reykholt from Magnus Palsson. All the timber and the stave church had been imported from Norway. Everything was still standing. So what was he worrying about? Certainly, it would have been more ostentatious to make Bessastadir his main seat and have the sea at his doorstep. But no, it was here in the hinterland that he felt most at home. The wind blew even more at Bessastadir. Snorre turned his eyes to the vapour that rose from the spring at Deildartunga a few hundred yards west of the ramparts. Behind it, he glimpsed the snow-covered mountains to the east. He'd made up his mind—he would never leave the Reykholt valley. The valley wasn't beautiful or remarkable in any way. Even the river Reykjadal wasn't notable for meanderings or waterfalls, unlike the Hvitá which became wild and treacherous each spring.

The estate was so quiet. No one had come to him and asked why the smith had ridden away. He closed the door and sat down at the long table.

He contemplated the passing moments. It was better than trying to fill them with something. Reluctantly, he picked up his quill and prepared to write. Why? To fill the moment anyway? He got nowhere. Not a single word on the calfskin, only a poorly executed sketch of an eye. He wanted to write about himself. If not, others would. Were there any grounds for trusting the other competent literates in the country? His nephew, Sturla Thordarson, wasn't wholly bereft of ability but that was all. He spoke little, and what he did say was often lost in his large brown beard. But he could write. Snorre lay down on the bunk next to the table. Was it true that if you lost contact with words, you gradually lost touch with people, too? No. He must write his own saga. It would begin: *There was a man called Snorre Sturlason.*

It had always been his habit to rest on the bunk. His eyes closed. He woke up when he landed on the floor. That had never happened before. What was to become of him if even his body wouldn't obey him? Deep inside, he knew that it never would again.

The thought of Margrete coming the next day made Snorre pick himself up, slightly too fast for his own good. There was a rushing at his temples. He held on to the table to steady himself. If only tomorrow would come! He felt dizzy. With faltering feet he made his way over to his bed and lay down fully clothed.

Snorre's need for Margrete was not solely as a lover. She had also defied him in a way that no one had ever done before. In her opinion, he'd been dishonest as a historian. According to Margrete, Snorre, and the Church as well, had betrayed their former allies in Constantinople during the Crusades. Margrete had been on a pilgrimage to Rome and had met a number of refugees from Constantinople and Byzantium. She knew what she was talking about. The first few times she'd levelled these accusations, Snorre had retorted that she couldn't possibly love him. She countered by saying that it was precisely because she loved him that she gave him her opinion.

The first time he'd met her, he had been less than impressed. He'd got the feeling that Margrete's husband,

Egil Halsteinson, had been pushing her onto him. Her husband had viewed Snorre as a powerful ally in several of the votes at the Althing. Snorre suspected that Margrete's lingering looks and generous laughter were prompted by his wealth and power.

In this saga about himself he would emphasize the most recent years. During the past five, there was nobody in the whole of Iceland who'd been more slandered than he had. Wasn't he, a man who was without doubt a capable writer, going to repudiate them? Posterity ought at least to have one sure source for who he was. Snorre had made many enemies after King Håkon killed Duke Skúli and he knew how he was going to deal with them. He would name them. First, he'd need to make these stay-at-homes aware of his position in the wider world. Snorre Sturlason wasn't a name known only in Iceland and in most of the Nordic countries; even in cities like Visby, Riga, Lübeck, Paris, Rome, Novgorod and Constantinople there were people who knew who he was. He understood perfectly that this wasn't due to his skill with the pen, but because of the political influence he wielded in Iceland and Norway. And this meant that his wealth and strategic abilities had become known far and wide. Those who had talked of lust for power and intrigue would be refuted. His influence stretched back far further than the twelve years he'd been Iceland's elected leader, its lawspeaker.

In papal circles in Rome they called him the 'prince of the sea'. The pope was constantly receiving missives from the archbishoprics of Nidaros and Lund, extolling his greatness. This was something his countrymen ought to know about. Even though he had written his most famous works when he'd been at the height of his powers, they had never been translated. They would be. Just wait. Maybe the

Younger Edda, the manual of instruction for poets with its summary of Nordic mythology, would be the first? Or *Heimskringla*, in which his saga of Saint Olaf pleased him the most?

He wouldn't spare his enemies. He knew quite well what was being said about him. It wasn't Snorre the historian and author they spoke ill of. It was the *cynical* father, the *grasping* stepfather, the *treacherous* minion of King Håkon who was slandered. And then there was the *philanderer* who seduced other men's wives. Not even the Sturlungs—his own kin—could be trusted! If he didn't name his enemies, the innocent might be suspected.

He would write about Orækja first. The relationship between him and his son was what most people talked about. He didn't attempt to hide how much he'd loved his firstborn, Little Jon. Snorre was forever reminding Orækja that Little Jon was a person everyone looked up to. Orækja must have noticed his father's earnestness whenever he spoke of how terribly he missed Little Jon.

How far could he go when writing about these highly confidential conversations with Orækja? He generally began them by stating that unless certain people were removed, their whole fortune could be at risk. When there was no more to add, he usually gave Orækja a pat on the shoulder and said, 'Don't get up to any mischief.' His son rarely knew what he meant. Orækja admired him and was grateful that his father was incapable of killing. Unlike Snorre, Orækja was almost always silent. He certainly wasn't talentless, but he'd never experienced the intoxicating feeling of wounding others. Orækja carried out the killings his father considered necessary to maintain or enlarge his and his family's power and wealth. His son was an extension of his arm. Just imagine if one day Orækja discovered that he didn't feel one iota of concern for him. Neatly, Snorre wrote his son's name. It stared back at him. He got no further.

This past year had seen his enemies multiply steadily.

Hallveig had been the richest woman in Iceland. After her death, Snorre had neglected to summon her sons, Klængr and Ormr, and divide her considerable estate with them. It all pointed to a desire to keep the whole inheritance for himself. His three sons-in-law, Gissur, Kolbeinn and Arni, had loved his daughters at first, and coveted the position that being married into his family afforded them. But after a few years they had become Snorre's enemies. They believed that he betrayed them once they were no longer of any use to him.

In return for a considerable sum and the title of feudal vassal, Snorre had pledged to bring Iceland under the Norwegian crown. It was more than twenty years since he'd given that undertaking. Three years previously, the king had asked Snorre's own brother Sighvatr and his nephew Sturla to bring Snorre to Norway. On that occasion, the king had entrusted the task to another, someone who was ambitious enough to want to be Iceland's mightiest.

And then there were the cuckolded husbands, like Torkild the smith and Margrete's man, Egil. The latter was a decayed, well-to-do farmer who had every reason to wish Snorre in his grave after a dishonourable death.

He wanted to write about all his enemies, but also about Margrete. They'd wasted so many years! He wanted to spend the rest of his life with her. He stretched in his bed. It creaked abjectly, it was the last thing he registered before falling asleep in the middle of the morning.

Snorre knew nothing of what was approaching. Two men crept along the wall of the house until they stood outside the room in which he slept. They could hear snoring. Cautiously, the door was opened. The taller of the two waited in the shadow for a moment while he scanned the farmyard. Warily, he approached Snorre. In his hand he held a club and a kerchief. The other man remained by the door. He kept a constant lookout. He'd never been to Reykholt before, and only seen Snorre from a distance. The poet was now sleeping deeply with his mouth open. The large man bent over Snorre and made sure that he really was asleep. Snorre turned his head to the side. The man at the door held his breath.

'The rope,' whispered the man by the bed.

The other nodded and came a couple of steps closer. Snorre raised his head and muttered something unintelligible. The man tightened his grip on the club. Just as Snorre turned his head the other way, they heard a shout from outside.

'There's someone there!'

Before Snorre was fully awake, the two men were out of the room and had closed the door carefully behind them. As they ran past Gyda, the youngest maidservant, the man who knew the place managed to inform her that if she or anyone else gave him away, they would be dead before nightfall. He whispered the name of the person who'd sent them. She went white. Snorre rose, shook his head, and padded to the door. Gyda was the only person in sight.

'Did I hear something?'

Gyda shook her head.

'I must have been dreaming.'

She nodded. She could see them astride their horses, waiting behind the church. As soon as Snorre was out of sight, they would ride back to their taskmaster.

Snorre ambled calmly over to the stable. He turned. Gyda had disappeared. In the semi-darkness he could make out fourteen horses. Kyrre had told him there were sixteen in all. There was only one horse he really knew. It was the nearest and smallest of them. He went up to it.

'Thank you, Sleipnir. Thank you for still being here,' he said.

The little horse lifted one of his front legs and moved his head from side to side. His forelock hung straight down. He whickered. Snorre spoke softly to him and patted him repeatedly. With more soothing words, he backed out of the stable. Nobody was waiting for him outside. Not even Kyrre, who was always supposed to keep an eye on the horses. Two men and two horses were missing. They would return, of course. He was sure of that. There were still plenty of people left, more than enough to run the estate properly. No doubt about it. Of course, it would be no easy matter to replace such a skilful smith as Torkild, but if the worst came to the worst, he could bring one over from Norway.

Snorre gazed up at the church, over towards the north gate. Through the open door of the little house next to it, he could see something moving. Was it the priest? It must be his imagination.

The day was already well advanced. Why weren't more people working? Would he have to shout for them? That would be a sight. Perhaps some of them already knew that Torkild had fled? What should he say to them? The sheep were approaching the farm in the hope of finding some juicy grass. They pressed their mouths to the dry ground as if nothing had happened. When they finally found something, they lowered their heads, grazed, lifted them again, chewed a couple of times on the scorched, yellow grass they'd found, before once more letting their heads sink with dignity and composure to search for a verdant dream with their tongues. This was what he would do—accept that people had run away and appear unruffled.

Were there as many cows in the meadow as there used to be? He stood still and began to count. With his left hand he shaded his eyes against the sun, which had speared the great, grey cloud with golden shafts. With his right hand he counted. He made it sixty. The small clouds vanished over the horizon with reefed sails. He had more cows at Bessastadir, but oughtn't there to be a few more here? Once again he began to count. Once again it came to sixty. Shouldn't there be sixty-two? Had two been stolen? There was no point in worrying when he couldn't even remember how many cows he had. He ought to be content with the fact that out there, within sight, there were sixty beasts. The figure was an easy one to remember—the same number of calfskins would make up half a book.

He must get on. With what? He ought to think about going indoors. Why not do something pleasant? He could lay out his finest clothes for tomorrow. His workers would certainly be nervous watching him wandering about their houses. They'd surely set about with their daily tasks as soon as he went in.

He must make them believe that Torkild had left with his permission. He could say that Torkild had been sent north on an errand. The clans were at war with each other, no one would dare to ask any questions. He must go inside. He must stop creeping round the houses. He must hold his head high. From now on he would smile and speak kindly to those he met.

As he turned towards his own door, he caught sight of Gyda again. She was walking rapidly away from the main house. Snorre called to her. She glanced quickly at him, and then looked straight ahead and continued walking, a little slower. Didn't she realize that he'd call her again?

'Gyda!'

She halted. Instead of coming over to him, she stood still. Her blonde hair hung in two thick plaits. Usually, the buxom girl had a becoming blush in her cheeks and a ready tongue. Now she was pale and silent. Snorre noticed that she didn't meet his eyes the way she usually did. He didn't mention the fact. Maybe she'd seen Torkild ride away? He didn't ask why she was in such a hurry. He must talk about something else. He began telling her what a burden Orækja was to him. She didn't contradict him.

He stood looking straight at Gyda as if he didn't know her. Was his son tired of him? When does a son have enough of his father? If he were out of the way, Orækja would inherit half of Reykholt, Bessastadir and a lot more besides.

His son always tried to reason the way he thought his father would, but the sentences eluded him before he managed to express anything of importance. Orækja was never satisfied with what finally came, faltering, from his lips. His father would have said it so much better. The idea that should have guided the words seemed so clear when he began to speak. But the words tumbled out in long, opaque sentences that got even longer when he saw his father shaking his head in mystification. It was the way it had always been, ever since Orækja's boyhood.

Snorre looked at Gyda. Yes, he wanted her. She was in her early twenties. He had noticed that some people around the estate teased her because she had a limp. Especially those who had little to do, or enjoyed an even lower status, like the two bondsmen who kept taunting her. And he'd caught them doing it! On both occasions she had begged him not to punish the cowardly bullies. How lovely she was, he mused, standing there with the weight on her left foot to ease her painful right leg.

He studied Gyda's face minutely. Had it not been for Margrete, the thought of her waiting for him in bed would have been delightful. Suddenly, the words poured out of him. He said that Oraekja had always had problems with girls, both servant girls and others. Ever since Oraekja's teens he'd noticed it. He had hardly even dared speak to girls. For years he'd only looked at them from afar. Looking at girls close up was as easy as winking, in his own opinion. But if one never went near them, the desire became almost *too* strong. When Oraekja saw one of the girls stoop to wash clothes in the stream, toss her hair or lift one leg over a horse's back, his face would become as round and still as a hole after a mouse had run down it.

Snorre had hoped these confidences would encourage Gyda to say something about Torkild, but her whole body spoke of wanting to move on. She said nothing, but simply contented herself with nodding or shaking her head, so Snorre gave up in the end. He took comfort in the fact that she probably hadn't seen anything at all.

Gyda and Kyrre talked about this strange conversation a few days later as they stood staring at the corpse of the great skald. Gyda related that Snorre's last words to her were that she should forget everything she'd heard. Then he'd smiled doubtfully, as if uncertain of her. Gyda was relieved that he hadn't quizzed her properly about what she'd seen. She made her way to the feasting hall as fast as she could, pretending she had things to do there.

Snorre went into the house. How restless he was! He stood by his desk. Should he even write about his children? Perhaps just Little Jon and Orækja? What about the other three? Not one of them could write themselves. What had he taught them? He'd been three years old when he'd sat in the saddle in front of his father, Sturla Thordarson, on their way from Hvammur in western Iceland to Oddi in the far south. Five days on horseback, travelling further and further away from his mother, Gudny. They were going to Jon Loptsson, the country's mightiest man back then in 1181. Jon had undertaken to bring up the youngest of Sturla's sons. Snorre and his father had crossed rivers, plains, meadows and valleys before they finally reached the man who, a few years later, was to teach him Latin and other languages, theology and geography, about the famous discussions at the University of Paris, astronomy and all the sciences of Córdoba, not to mention Constantinople, to which Icelanders and Norwegians had been travelling for several hundred years.

It was at Oddi that he'd first heard of Jerusalem, the river Jordan, Jericho and Rome. And London, the Silk Route from Beijing and Dublin—imagine going there and studying the language and history of the Celts! At Oddi he'd learnt to write, his body bent over the calfskin and the goose quill in his right hand. It began with a single letter, then several, an entire word, a sentence. It was at Jon's that he was able to read the books that were available in Iceland. His foster father had got him Aesop's Fables, Donatus' and Priscian's Latin grammars. The *Physiologus* which told of animals, both those he'd seen, and animals he'd never even heard of. The *Elucidarium* and several treatises on theology, the story of the people of Troy, the history of the Apostles Peter and Paul, the dictionary, world history and much more besides.

He glanced over at his own copy of the *Physiologus*, and read the introduction which referred to the Latin title, Bestiary. He began leafing through it at random. The pages that revealed themselves were the ones he'd tuned to most often. BEE: Representation of the Holy Spirit, lives on the scent of flowers, the symbol of purity and abstinence. BUCK: Rutting, butting, always eager to mate. BUCK'S BLOOD: Can dissolve diamonds. ROCK CRYSTAL: Like the diamond, it is the sun's counter-agent to the Devil. And here! UNICORN: A strange creature whose horn some mistake for that of the narwhal. He raised his chin and took in the drawing of the unicorn, with the horn coming out of its forehead and its four legs. He didn't know anybody who'd seen one. When the unicorn spies a virgin, it goes straight up to her, lays the young girl down and penetrates her maidenly parts, he read. DREAM: The winged genius of dream. CROCODILE: A creature that has clambered out of the primeval slime. LION: Just like the eagle, the lion can stare straight into the sun without narrowing its eyes. It sweeps away its footprints with its tail. He thumbed rapidly back to the illustration of the leopard, before leafing forward to PARROT and PEACOCK. Here, his eye caught the words VANITY and GOD'S EYE. He looked over at the miserable eye he'd drawn on the calfskin. Obviously, there wasn't going to be any more writing today. Today, he reassured himself, as if there would be plenty of days to follow. He glanced at the entries TIGER, TORTOISE and TURTLE before laying the great volume aside. What had he given his own children?

Breathless, Snorre seated himself at the long table again. It would be wonderful to have a visit from Margrete. Provided she didn't spend the entire time talking about Constantinople and 1204. The fact that she was so overwhelmingly right didn't help matters. He saw her face clearly in his mind's eye. Tomorrow she would come, get off her horse, embrace him, sweep her hair from her forehead and fix him with her green eyes. He fetched the hat he would wear when she arrived, brushed it and held it in his hand. He opened the door and went out onto the doorstep. The hat in his hand was like some imploring gesture to the heavens. He went indoors again and laid it down.

He'd forgotten to cut his hair. He felt it. He took the longest of the three pairs of scissors on the table, went across to the hearth, squatted and looked at himself in the new, shiny cooking pot. With wary fingers he manoeuvred the scissors to the long hair at the nape of his neck and hesitated a few seconds before cutting, once, twice, three times, four times. He laid the scissors down and examined himself for a long time before rising and brushing away the blonde, grey and white hairs. He crouched and gazed at his reflection again. She couldn't be too displeased.

Now he must speak to Kyrre! He felt cold. He put his blue cloak on over his coat. He fastened the buckle at his shoulder. With long strides, Snorre walked towards the barn where Kyrre was generally to be found. He stood in the yard and shouted for the stable lad. He glanced first at the barn, and then at the stable. He normally curried and tended the horses out of doors. He couldn't see the horses or the stable lad. What was the matter with Kyrre, the barn door was open! A fine thing if the stock found their way inside and began eating the winter fodder. Snorre shut the door. But what was that movement just over by the corner of the barn? It must be Kyrre. Was he hiding? Snorre walked as fast as he could. He was panting, and he waited until his breathing returned to normal before slipping round the corner. No one there. Could he have been mistaken? He stole round the next corner. A twig snapped. Snorre tried to move even faster round the south corner. Kyrre was lying on the ground clutching his knee.

'Why are you hiding?'

'I didn't know it was you.'

'Why is no one working outside?'

'Aren't they?'

'Important people are coming tomorrow.'

'Oh, very well.'

'Where did Torkild the smith go?'

'I don't know.'

'Wouldn't Torkild have told you?'

There was silence.

'You're lying!' Snorre shouted.

Kyrre shook his head even more emphatically. Snorre eyed him. Kyrre lowered his eyes.

'Maybe one of the others knows where he is?'

Snorre turned and went indoors.

He had to lay out his best clothes. Tomorrow she'd be here. It was six years since he'd first met Margrete, and now she was coming to Reykholt for the first time. He picked up the longest pair of thin scissors which lay next to his comb on the long table. He trimmed his beard a little, without looking at himself in the shiny pot.

No sooner had he reached for the comb, than the thought of Oraekja forced itself on him. His son was capable of ruining anything. Snorre propped his head heavily on his hand. The elbow pressed on the table top. How fond he'd been of Jon and Hallbera, the legitimate children he'd had with Herdis, his first wife. He missed them.

Is there anything worse than surviving your own children? Jon was named after Snorre's foster father, Jon Loptsson. Little Jon had been pale and sickly. And how slowly he grew! Neither Herdis nor Snorre knew the reason for it. On one occasion during his morning change, Herdis had called the baby *Murtr*, and the nickname 'Small Fry' had stuck to him for the rest of his life.

At the age of eighteen, Jon had been murdered.

The previous year, Snorre had promised the Norwegian chieftains that he would send his son to Norway as a guarantee that he, Snorre, would create peace between the Icelanders and the Norwegians. The inhabitants of Oddi and the merchants of Bjørgvin dominated the trade with Iceland. The country had hardly any merchant vessels of its own. Trade with Norway was crucial to the Icelanders. Peace there was, and Jon returned home bearing the praise of duke and king alike. How proud he'd been of the boy! Jon wasn't the sort to gloat and brag about his successes. Small Fry simply stated that he'd done what his father had asked of him. Nothing more. He'd opened his arms, looked at his father and smiled. What a time that had been! Snorre had felt himself Iceland's richest man in every sense of the word.

A week after Jon returned from Norway, he'd knocked at Snorre's door. Even after Small Fry had been admitted, he remained standing by the door. In a low voice, the boy told him his errand. His father sat writing, engrossed in his own thoughts.

'That was no excuse!' Snorre said aloud to himself. Jon explained that he wanted to marry Helga Sæmundardottir of Oddi. Snorre nodded and stroked his nose with the feather of his pen. In an even quieter voice, Jon asked if he mightn't have a dowry and maybe the farm at Stafaholt. It seemed only reasonable after the service he'd done his father in Norway. Snorre made no reply. He held the quill calmly, lowered his head and went on writing. His gaze wandered between the letters, the penknife, the inkwell and the charcoal pencil at the edge of the parchment, as if nothing had been said.

Jon left Reykholt without a word. He rode to his grandmother and Uncle Thordr, and they gave him what he wanted. The shame of it. Snorre had tried to put things right. Of course Jon could have Stafaholt and the means he'd requested. Snorre asked Jon to return. Surely Jon knew he was his father's favourite? But Jon hadn't wanted to meet his father.

His eyes filled. He rose, banging his clenched fist on the table.

Jon sailed back to Norway. He was well received there. Duke Skúli made him a retainer, and he met King Håkon at Bjørgvin. They saw eye to eye. Their conversations were so relaxed, and the harmony between his son and the king was so great that Snorre saw how different his life could have been if he'd learnt to value Jon's qualities. At Bjørgvin, Jon shared accomodation with Gissur Thorvaldsson, who later married his half-sister, Ingibjørg. One evening, Jon and Gissur returned to their lodging accompanied by a stranger. They were as drunk as lords. It was Jon who'd offered the stranger a roof. Kind, generous Jon.

Late that night, there was a fight. The guest, Olafr Svartskald, struck Jon with an axe and made off. Jon didn't consider the wound serious. A week later he was dead.

'Jon!' cried Snorre.

He found it hard to breathe. His heart was pounding. He opened the door to get some fresh air. The pregnant grey cat lay outside. He kicked it away. He gazed across

Reykholt. Over there, two people, at least, had begun working. He couldn't make out who they were. They seemed to be digging a long, narrow trench. He glimpsed the pool, the only place where his thoughts could find solace. He remembered Gissur Thorvaldsson's bowed head, that evening he'd come to relate what had happened to Small Fry. The words, those helpless words, the voice choked with weeping, the way Gissur gasped for breath, the way they'd embraced, the curses they'd expended on Olafr, the man who'd repaid Jon's kindness with an axe, how they'd talked over one another trying to recall all the good things about the person they'd both loved.

Snorre reached for the Byzantine pottery vase which stood on the table. Margrete had given it to him. The subject was outlined in black on a white background. He could make out a lighthouse painted in red behind a woman and a man. The motif was taken from the myth about the lovers Hero and Leander. Margrete had explained that the lighthouse stood on a little island in the Bosporus Strait off Constantinople.

Where would Torkild find work now? With Orækja? Was that how the land lay? Outdoors, he could see Gyda who, five days later, would run distractedly round the farmyard shouting that he'd been murdered.

It was ten years since the two children who'd meant the most to him had died. First Little Jon and then Hallbera. She'd died of disease. Hallbera had first married Arni 'the Fickle' Magnusson, but later divorced him and become Kolbeinn's wife. Snorre fathered Thordis, Ingibjørg and Orækja with different women outside wedlock.

He fetched his best clothes and laid them carefully on the bench. He placed his smart hat on top of the pile. He smiled. At all times, in all weathers, no matter where he was, he thought of Margrete. The sun had penetrated the layer of cloud. He went over to the desk. Was that something burnt he could smell? He looked over at the hearth. The fire hadn't been lit today. Was it coming from outside? Should he go out? No, the others could take care of it.

Snorre wanted to avoid Arnbjørn the priest—he was capable of wittering on about trivialities for hours, as if eternity had been created solely for him. Even so, he was the only person at Reykholt Snorre could converse with about the great thinkers, about the kings of Norway and of other lands, and the Bible. As well as being well read, Arnbjørn was well travelled.

Snorre hadn't set eyes on him since he'd caught Arnbjørn in the pool three days before. Of course it was embarrassing, but Snorre found it strange that the priest should hide himself away. One evening when they'd been drinking and playing chess, Snorre had let drop the secret nobody else on the estate was privy to. That the underground tunnel between the main house and the pool wasn't the only one. There were several covert passages beneath Reykholt which he could use if danger threatened. After Sturla and Sighvatr's attack, the ramparts around Reykholt had been reinforced but most of the effort had gone into this underground network. The priest had sworn never to divulge the secret. Snorre regretted saying so much to Arnbjørn. There was only one way to keep Arnbjørn quiet. He'd have to be killed.

Snorre undressed as he walked across the flagstones to the circular pool which he'd constructed along Roman lines. He was alone there as he lowered his body into the warm water which welled over the pool's stone surround and into the grass. He gave a deep sigh. Snorre loved sinking into the naturally heated water, whatever the time of year. He'd built the pool with his own hands. He was proud of the fact. He had named the pool *Snorrelauget*—Snorre's Bath.

Orækja seldom asked about his mother. Whenever he did, his father tried to change the subject. Snorre had allowed his son to grow up at Reykholt. He didn't dare let him out of his sight. How many times had he considered denying paternity, renouncing him and telling him to leave and never come back! He raised his arm and used the palm of his hand to make small waves in the water, which slapped against the sand-coloured stone round the edge of the pool. The water assumed its glassy smoothness. He looked down at it. In both features and physique, he resembled Orækja.

Snorre remembered his first sight of Orækja. Orækja's mother, Thurid, raised the baby towards him. He was amazed at how much hair the creature had. She asked if he couldn't see it was a boy. He drew out his reply, and she pushed the little bundle up to his face. Snorre stared at the unkempt hair. He didn't register that the baby was crying at the top of its voice. He examined the small eyes. The open mouth was of no interest to him. The eyes were closed, squeezed tight in rage at stomach pains or hunger. For an instant, the tiny thing opened its eyes. Most people would have said the moment was barely perceptible, but it was long enough for the child's parents to be in no doubt. Orækja was Snorre's son.

The relationship between Snorre and Orækja had worsened considerably after they sailed home from Norway together two years before. Snorre squirmed at the memory of what had occurred.

The journey had started peacefully enough. During the week before setting sail on his last journey back to

Iceland in 1239, he'd experienced several lengthy nightmares. On the day of departure, in the bright morning light, with the sea a flat calm around the isle of Munkholm, off Nidaros, he heard a scream and a clearly audible voice ordering him to stay. He was explicitly warned of what he should already have known, that he had countless enemies in Iceland. This made quite an impression, for a short while. An unpleasant thought or two was stirred up and caused some disharmony, but immediately settled again, just as dogs and cats curl up together round the hearth.

Snorre didn't ask himself where the voice came from. He was too determined to ignore what it had to say for that.

He was standing with his foot on the gunwale. Down on the beach, a couple of women had lifted their skirts and were pissing on the nets to bring the fishermen luck. Behind the women lay the town of Nidaros and the country he would never see again. He gave his orders in a clear voice and hoisted sail, with a retinue of forty men, two women and Orækja on board.

As a rule he was considered a ditherer, a man who put off making any decision for as long as possible. His money and literary skills would see him through this time too, he believed. Despite an unprecedented number of unseasonable storms in the Norwegian Sea, Snorre insisted that he must return to the island out in the Atlantic. At all costs, Snorre wanted to go back to Iceland, the little nation under the North Star, the land of fire and ice. He must travel home to cling on to what was left of his power and property.

Try as they might to dissuade him, he would defy every warning. The last time he'd sailed from Norway to Iceland, twenty years before, the mast had snapped. Everything was pointing to a horrendous journey with storms, violent squalls, boiling waves, fang-like crescents of foam, broken oars, shredded sails and men overboard, and himself being bashed on the back of the head by the boom and falling into the water, his mouth and belly filling with brine before he sank to the bottom of the sea. It didn't happen. In typical fashion, many of his contemporaries would have said, the storm abated just as he set sail. From the moment he went on board, it was as if the sea had never known a wave.

For several days, he ate and drank with zest, heartiness and satisfaction, and behaved with the utmost consideration towards the women on board. He shrugged his shoulders when he was asked if he'd had a visitation from Almighty God, telling him that the weather would change. His quizzical expression showed that he took the fine weather for granted, like someone who's used to getting what he wants. During the voyage they didn't meet a single ship. The only thing they saw was a good deal of driftwood. Father and son spoke laughingly of King Håkon, who had refused them permission to sail back to Iceland, and of how much they missed their homeland.

Two nights out from Iceland, it happened. Banks of fog had made it more difficult to navigate using the stars, and Orækja began criticizing his father's navigational instructions to the mate. Those who heard Orækja's words thought he spoke amicably, unusually clear and calm. The mate said nothing, but it wasn't hard to see that he was inclined to follow Orækja's advice. The evening was almost hot. Is anything more portentous than a dead, calm sea? Snorre regarded the mate before again focusing his attention on his son. He shouted. The people gazed questioningly at one another before turning their eyes back to Snorre and his son. They were frightened Orækja would fly into a rage.

Suddenly, his father fell silent and stared at him. Orækja responded with a look that was full of surprise. The son shook his head, as if wanting to tell his father that he'd misunderstood, and then stood still.

With purposeful stride, Snorre went aft and fetched a coil of rope. He ordered his son to sit down.

'I don't know what you might be capable of this far out to sea.'

Without any sign of protest or resistance, Orækja sat down on the deck. Snorre told him to stretch his wrists behind his neck. And so, with his wrists on the thwart and his back towards the bow of the boat, Orækja was bound fast. The mate was given the job of lashing the strong arms to the thwart. Snorre went to the helm, looked out across the sea and steered the boat himself. Orækja was left sitting in the same position all night, while the others slept round him. The only one who stayed awake was his father. Father and son exchanged no words whatever. It was early morning before the mate was permitted to release Orækja. Nobody said a word about what had happened to either Snorre or Orækja.

When they sighted Iceland in the distance, the younger elements aboard began to shout and sing. A day later they reached home at last. At first they saw a couple of gulls, then innumerable gulls and, finally, the odd sea eagle gliding high above them all. The well-known outline of the Vestmann Islands grew ever clearer through the mist. The crew thanked the higher powers for allowing them to see once again the green fields that ended abruptly in steep cliffs. Some clasped their hands and mumbled.

The boat tied up at the quay. Orækja bounded ashore. Just like a child trying to be first, he scrambled down shoving two older men aside. Snorre turned away in shame, and breathed hard. Then Snorre's horse was led to the gangplank. Was he really so small? Snorre stood on the deck and looked once more at the little Iceland pony with his thick, brown coat, as if to reassure himself that it was indeed Sleipnir who was standing there. He negotiated the gangplank, his back bent, his head full of countless images of sky and sea, the motion of the prow, the predictability of the horizon.

As soon as Snorre was ashore, he shouted to Kyrre to take his pack. Then he mounted Sleipnir. Now and then his feet brushed the ground. It began to rain. That day Snorre kept to the saddle as long as it was light. Orækja rode a little way behind his father.

About half a mile before their paths diverged, Orækja rode up beside his father. Snorre looked straight ahead or down at Sleipnir's mane. Father and son rode side by side in silence. As soon as Orækja saw the path to Stafaholt, he dug his heels into his black horse and rode ahead of Sleipnir. His father didn't raise his eyes. His son pulled up hard in front of him. Snorre raised his head a fraction. They were alone. Snorre rode right up to his son. Orækja could have reached out an arm and pulled Snorre from his horse. He was strong and agile. He could easily have killed Snorre with his bare hands or with the sword that hung at his thigh. The Norwegian king and a number of Iceland's worthies would have thanked him. The horses nuzzled each other. The men could hear each other's breath. Snorre glanced apathetically at Orækja's horse. The son tried to catch his father's eye. Orækja let his right hand drop from the reins. Quickly, he held it out: 'Forgive me, Father, you were right.'

His father was still staring at the horse.

'Back there, on board,' Orækja added before withdrawing his hand.

Orækja cleared his throat and mumbled a hesitant farewell as he turned the horse into the path for Stafaholt.

As soon as his son was out of sight, Snorre patted Sleipnir, spoke friendly words to the horse and rode towards Reykholt. He put the horse into a running walk before trotting him, and then urged him into a running walk again. He talked to himself about Orækja, and the horse laid back his ears to catch the familiar sound of Snorre's voice. Sleipnir whinnied. The rain ceased. The sky went an indigo blue, before taking on a violet, and then a light red hue which cut right through to the underside of the roof of clouds, behind shafts of gold, until mellow darkness enveloped the landscape, the horse and rider.

He rode to his wife, Hallveig Ormsdottir, who'd been staying at Breidabolstadir with her sons, Klængr and Ormr, while he'd been in Norway. Hallveig rode back to Reykholt with Snorre.

Snorre stretched his arms and gripped the edge of the pool. The stones rubbed against his head. He tried to keep his hips up in the water. His sturdy legs forced his body back into the upright position. His feet were soon on the stony bottom again, like two heavy, white anchors of flesh and bone. Did his ankles feel a bit less swollen in the pool?

When it came to the jobs that were cloaked in darkness, the ones that Snorre either couldn't or wouldn't carry out, he conjured up his son just as one conjures the Devil. He was dependent on Orækja.

The only occasions on which Orækja glimpsed anything that resembled relief in his father's features was when he reported that he'd neutralized an enemy. Snorre never thanked him. He had one less problem, but he'd soon express anxiety over other enemies and rivals. He was never completely satisfied.

'Is there anything else I can do, Father?' asked his son. And each time, his son's subservience and eagerness to please irritated Snorre, even though he would need Orækja's services again soon enough.

Snorre wiggled his fingers under the water. He turned quickly. The houses stood there as ever, thank God.

Orækja was no schemer. His father often admonished him for his gullibility where people he wanted to be on good terms with were concerned. He was a brutal bumbler. If the object was to break a man's little finger, he would break all his fingers, then his wrist and forearm. Snorre slapped the water with the flat of his hand.

'He's his father's hatchet,' was what his nephew Sturla used to say. Even when Orækja was a child, his father felt relief every time he was absent from Reykholt.

Snorre felt the bottom beneath his feet and took a step forward. The water was up to his chest. He plunged his head into the warm water. He held his breath under water for a few seconds before he straightened again and tossed his hair back, making the spray fly.

Margrete lay a day's ride from Reykholt. Her husband Egil lay on top of her, groaning and kissing the freckles on her nose. She closed her eyes and thought of Snorre waiting at Reykholt. Nothing can rankle quite like marital bliss.

That same day, King Håkon arrived at Nidaros. The bishop's valet ran up to the king. Before the king was able to enquire, the servant informed him that they'd had no news of Snorre. The task hadn't been accomplished. Orækja approached Reykholt at full gallop. Three days earlier, a ship had arrived on Iceland's west coast. Three emissaries from the pope in Rome were aboard. They were to hand Snorre a letter.

Snorre sat in the pool and wondered where Orækja could be. Kyrre, who had watched Snorre going to and from his daily bath, was nevertheless surprised at the size of the old poet when he lay naked on the grey sail a few days later, his skin becoming blotched with blue marks.

It was Snorre who'd arranged the marriage between Orækja and Arnbjørg, Kolbeinn's sister. It would bind the Åsbirning clan closer to the Sturlungs, Snorre had thought. Neither Arnbjørg nor Orækja were consulted beforehand. His father had hoped that marriage might be a calming influence on the then twenty-seven-year-old because Arnbjørg was both strong and unafraid. But Orækja got wilder. And Arnbjørg? She was thoroughly supportive and loyal to her husband. She always defended his actions and tended his wounds with the care of a heaven-sent nurse. At last Orækja had found a true mainstay. Several times Orækja had said that she was the only person in the whole of Iceland who understood him. Snorre's wise choice of spouse for him was yet another reason for Orækja to love and honour his father.

Whenever Snorre had tried to make his son see reason, Arnbjørg reminded him that he hadn't come to their wedding. Nor had Snorre kept his word to her brother, Kolbeinn, when he'd married Hallbera, that they'd have the farm of Mel. Immediately after Orækja's wedding, Snorre needed help with the Vatnsfirding clan near Isafjord in the far north. His son refused him nothing. Snorre wanted to make certain that the taxes were collected punctually, and it was far enough away for there to be quiet at Reykholt for a while. He needed some peace to write.

No sooner had Orækja arrived at Isafjord, than Snorre began to hear about various murders and plunderings. As if that weren't enough, Orækja claimed that he'd done it all on his father's orders. Snorre hadn't asked for anyone to be killed on this occasion.

Snorre gazed down at his hairy stomach. His navel was invisible. How he regretted sending Orækja north! Should he have gone himself? He didn't possess his son's strength at the decisive moment. He smacked his hand on the water. The drops were visible on the stones around him. Snorre stared at the water running off his straggly, unkempt beard.

Was the wind direction misleading him? Was the burning coming from some way off? With much effort, he got out of the pool. Water cascaded around him. He walked naked across the yard and past the grindstone. Smoke was coming from Torkild's toolstore. Was there someone there? Now he'd catch them. He didn't even have time to feel apprehensive about being unarmed. Snorre threw open the door. There was no one there! A small fire had been lit on the ground. It hadn't caught properly. He smothered it with a spade. He was just about to shout. He'd get everyone at Reykholt together and ask who was responsible. Where was Orækja? Was he trying to drive his own father off the estate and take over himself? He peered out of the door. There wasn't a soul to be seen.

Snorre dressed and walked purposefully to the stable. Now he must try to find Orækja. He mounted Sleipnir and rode slowly away from Reykholt. His head and chin were high, his back was straight and his chest thrust out, while his elbows were tight against his body. But where should he ride? Once through the gate he increased his pace. He pressed his ankles into the horse's sides, at the same time shortening the reins to keep control. With hands and wrists relaxed, he sent his signals to Sleipnir's mouth and muzzle. His thumbs were turned up, whilst his fingers worked as if trying to squeeze water out of a cloth. If he wanted more speed, he spoke kindly but firmly to the horse. Sleipnir was happiest at this easy trot. Even though most Iceland ponies possess a good sense of place, Sleipnir was in a class of his own. Several times he'd found his way home to Reykholt alone. A fortnight before, he'd escaped from the stable at Borg. Snorre rode past the open horse shelter, surrounded by its large enclosure for winter use.

As soon as Reykholt had disappeared from sight, he stopped. A horse's skull lay on the path before him. He hadn'd seen it before. That was strange. He'd ridden past this same spot not very long ago. The joins in the skull looked like a jagged seam between the plates of bone. He got off his horse, raised the skull with both hands and examined it. Sand poured out as he tilted it. He replaced it on the path and remounted Sleipnir. There was still a little of the day left. It would be a while before the last remnants of the light would spread across the plain behind him and recede to the outer rim of the world in a cold blue. And it would be even longer before the birdsong subsided in the dark bushes around him.

Snorre clicked his tongue and moved Sleipnir on. The fine dust covered the horse's fetlocks. He clamped the heels of his boots against Sleipnir's flanks. He leant forward in the saddle with the reins in his left hand before the legs began to gallop.

Snorre wanted to believe that the horse's skull was a coincidence, that it was a joke and not a warning. Or, if it *was* a warning, that it had nothing to do with him. That was what it must be, he mumbled to Sleipnir. His horse was the only thing he really thought he knew. When the mares were in heat, Snorre would talk to him in a deep voice, without lying. And when Sleipnir, on rare occasions, was angry, Snorre talked him round with biblical turns of phrase. The horse understood this.

Maybe Sleipnir knew where Orækja was? Orækja had ridden hereabouts often enough. The horse stopped dead, reared and neighed. Within the cage of his ribs, his fleshy heart pumped blood around his tensed body. His strong thigh bones succeeded in keeping his body upright with the aid of taut sinews and muscles. They were like hawsers that stretched and contracted over bones and kneecaps. The two hoofprints where all the weight had been resembled wells in the dusty ground. His forelock swung from side to side above the large eyes—two ardent, agitated globes in which the world burnt. The fatty cushions of his muzzle revealed a palisade of teeth. Snorre stroked Sleipnir's head energetically. He nearly fell, but managed to cling on. His voice calm, he tried to talk to Sleipnir. When at last he could dismount, he found a horse's skull on a stake in front of him.

Snorre shouted his son's name.

Snorre got into the saddle rueing the day, two years before, when he'd sent Orækja to deal with Kolbeinn. To be sure, Kolbeinn hadn't fulfilled his part of the distribution of Hallbera's estate, but it was more than ten years since she'd died. One element of this had been Snorre's own greed but he had no awareness of this himself. What filled him with anxiety was that the affair could, without his knowledge, have driven Orækja over to Kolbeinn's or Thordr's sides. None of them had much to thank Snorre for. Thordr had never believed Snorre's excuses. He knew that.

Orækja had set out with an army of poor peasants, well armed and hungry for easy booty. When Kolbeinn's estate finally hove into view, a messenger from Snorre came galloping up. There were a number of horses in front of the main building. Many of the hungry men fantasized about what the storehouse they could see in the distance might contain.

Fifteen men had drawn their bows in front of Orækja's horse when the messenger handed over the leather container. He opened it quickly. Orækja regarded the messenger and the bowmen by turns. He reread the letter. There could be no doubt. It was his father's handwriting and signature. If he killed the messenger, he could tell his father that he'd never received the countermand. Orækja turned to his bowmen. He ordered them to lower their bows. One of the men asked if this meant they weren't going to set light to their arrows now. Orækja punched him in the face. Blood ran from the lean, brown-haired youth's split lip. Were they simply to walk away from the great farm that lay right before them? They could make a big killing with hardly any resistance. What was Orækja thinking of?

They had galloped all night in order to surprise Kolbeinn. They hadn't eaten for twelve hours. Their horses were exhausted and steaming with sweat. The messenger had changed horses three times himself just to catch up with them. Orækja gazed out over the assembly. They were waiting for the order to attack. Orækja raised his arm. There was silence. The outline of the low buildings was even clearer in the dawn light. He raised his voice: 'We'll attack Thordr instead.' The men looked at one another in disbelief. The messenger and Orækja's men all jabbered simultaneously. What was he talking about? He repeated his order and promised them food before the sun was halfway across the sky. Grudgingly, they lowered their bows and mounted their horses again.

Snorre shook his head despondently. It was deeply unfair that both outsiders and members of his own family maintained that he was the one who'd told his son to attack Thordr. How ridiculous! It could hardly have suited him less. He had absolutely no motive for getting Orækja to do it. Had he been consulted, he would have foreseen the catastrophe. He could see his brother in his mind's eye. Thordr's face was so small that it must be painful to smile with it. The relationship between him and his brother had never been cordial. If he didn't manage to chronicle this event, the Sturlungs would be split for decades to come.

'To Thordr!' Orækja had shouted. His voice cracked. Everyone could tell that his words carried no conviction. A few days later, Thordr managed to divide Orækja's force. He took thirty of his men prisoner, disarmed them, took their horses and hanged their two commanders in front of them. Orækja and the rest of his men were put to flight.

Snorre turned all his wrath on his son. This hurt Orækja. Before the sun was at its zenith, Orækja decided that he would do everything he could to please his father. He would try to placate Sighvatr, his other uncle. Sighvatr rebuffed him curtly and told Orækja to stay near his father, who was then in the south at Bessastadir. Orækja took his words at face value and rode with the remnant of his band towards Bessastadir. Snorre thought his son was coming to kill him, and fled on horseback up to Borgarfjord to gather people against Orækja. It took some days for Snorre to realize that he'd been mistaken.

To get a bit of peace from Orækja, he'd presented him with the farm of Stafaholt. Perhaps now he'd have time to write? Surely, after all this, Orækja would manage to remain calm, even if he hadn't before? Without seeking advice from his father or anyone else, he again rode north to Sighvatr. Oræksja felt he hadn't managed to have a proper conversation with his uncle. Sighvatr stood in the yard, unarmed, talking to the smith.

His uncle was completely unaware that Oræksja had taken up position right behind him. Oræksja whispered Sighvatr's name, and Sighvatr nodded because he assumed it was one of his servants pestering him. His uncle was deep in discussion with the smith about how many swords were to be forged. Talking to the smith wasn't something that could be done in a trice. The length, width and handle had to be considered. Sighvatr had some knowledge of the craft. In his youth he'd worked as a smith for six months. Without turning, he said he didn't want to be disturbed. Oræksja repeated his uncle's name. The smith glanced behind him. He went as white as a sheet. Sighvatr turned his head. Then dropped his hand to the sword which wasn't there. Oræksja smiled, not out of malice, but because he thought it would put his uncle in a good humour. Sighvatr slapped his thigh as soon as he realized he had no sword. The smith raised his hammer. Oræksja explained that he'd come hoping for friendship with Sighvatr. The uncle looked his nephew up and down. Was this vicious ninny trying to make a fool of him? Oræksja was wearing his sword in his belt. He wasn't making the least move to grasp the weapon. He was serious! What could he do without losing too much face? He nodded as his nephew jabbered, promising peace and toleration.

'That's enough now,' said his uncle.

Sighvatr stalked out of the forge right in the middle of one of Oræksja's convoluted explanations. In the yard outside, forty of Oræksja's men had congregated. Sighvatr considered them. They were thin and undernourished. Most of them were bondsmen. His uncle smiled at Oroekja and opened his arms. With exultation in his voice he announced that he would invite them all to a great celebration.

'As soon as I saw you, Uncle, I knew you'd welcome us. This is too generous, but thanks anyway,' Oroekja said.

Lamb was roasted and covered with mint, ale was brought out; sides of pork with apples, berries and fruit as well as hazelnut cakes were placed on the table. Oroekja's men got drunk. Oroekja helped himself greedily to everything that was provided. Sighvatr kept asking if he wouldn't have more. Sighvatr was drinking water. As his uncle sat looking down the long table, a man appeared out of the darkness. He was like a shadow flitting along the side wall, and then he stopped under the torch by Sighvatr, bent and whispered in his ear. Oroekja hadn't noticed the incident. Snorre would surely be pleased that he was settling things with his uncle, he surmised.

The sad thing is that fools are so naive and cocksure, and wise men so full of doubt.

Several times during the meal, Oroekja asked his uncle whether they couldn't be reconciled and become friends like in the old days. The man who'd earlier whispered in Sighvatr's ear was a messenger from his son Sturla, who was only a couple of hours away with a hundred men. Sturla had been on a pilgrimage to Rome and favourable winds in the Norwegian Sea had brought him home faster than expected. Suddenly the door was flung open.

Sturla positioned himself between his father and Oroekja. He demanded that Oroekja and his men leave the estate.

'Now, when things are so pleasant?' Oroekja asked.

There was silence.

'Aren't you going to say anything?' Orækja said to his uncle.

Several of Orækja's men got up, some ran from the room and finally Orækja, drunk and perspiring, left the table and went out into the darkness beneath the stars. He felt himself being hoisted onto his horse, heard a slap on the rump directly behind him and then realized with icy clarity that he was on a wild gallop to nowhere.

It took days for Orækja to gather his men again. He went to Isafjord in the north, far away from his father and the rest of his family. To get money he levied heavy taxes on the peasants. If they didn't pay, their farms and crops were burnt. It wasn't many months before Snorre was given to understand that the peasants would start destroying the Sturlungs' property all round the island if his son's rampages didn't cease. After this incident, Snorre knew that he couldn't control his son any longer.

It shouldn't have been difficult to dispose of Orækja. Anybody would willingly have done the deed if he hadn't been so unpredictable. No one but Arnbjørg would have missed him. Snorre had asked her once if she really loved Orækja. She had looked Snorre in the eye and replied: 'Thou shalt honour thy husband!' It was like a sentence she'd willingly accepted. Snorre was sure of one thing—he was incapable of killing Orækja himself.

Snorre rode in a wide circle around the estate. He wanted to keep Reykholt under surveillance. They'd arrived at where the Hvitá was at its broadest, and Snorre felt sure Orækja was close by. Sleipnir stood uneasily. He wanted to cross the river. Snorre brought Sleipnir to the bank, got off the horse, undressed and hauled himself up again. He held his clothes and bow above his head. The belt carrying his sword and knife was strapped around his waist.

In the middle of the river Sleipnir swam a few strokes, snorting and stretching his neck out of the water with his tail rippling behind him. The current carried them a little way downstream, as Snorre leant forward, speaking calmly into the horse's ear. Sleipnir soon had firm ground under his hooves. They rode against the stream to a bank of gravel. He could find no trace of any foot- or hoofprint. They turned once they were on dry land. The drought of the past few months had left the river tamer then normal. Sleipnir began to gallop across the stony river bank. The horse set off in the sunny afternoon air, and water ran from his mane.

Just as Snorre had decided to change direction, he caught sight of fresh tracks. He let the horse slacken his pace. It was travelling over dense, dry bog grasses. Far away he saw a pale half-moon cutting the sky. He followed the tracks. Sleipnir's rhythm slowed. Snorre, watchful, held the reins. It must be Orækja. He would surprise him. He would say that he wasn't in the least bit frightened of him. He would dismount and do something he hadn't done since Orækja's boyhood—he would box his ears.

The campfire had only just been deserted. There were tracks of two horses. He inspected the fire and trod out the embers, loosened Sleipnir's stirrups, mounted the horse and rode homewards. With the years, it had become more difficult to concentrate at his desk. He thought best when he was on Sleipnir's back. He'd never seen Orækja so clearly in his mind's eye before.

Snorre rode back to Reykholt as fast as he could. He spoke familiarly to Sleipnir all the while, in much the same way as he addressed his dead wife when he visited her grave. Quietly and confidentially. Talking to her hadn't been easy when she'd been alive. The ground reverberated under the horse's hooves, his mane was like ears of corn in a storm, his tail flew behind him like the wildest spume. For a moment he released the reins and smacked Sleipnir's rump with his hand.

While abroad, he'd had the chance to buy a real Arab several times. These horses were supposed to be bigger, faster and more supple than Iceland ponies. They said that it was largely due to them that the Crusaders had lost the first time. But he was sure they could never make up for the sense, endurance and thick coat of the Iceland pony. And what was the point of having horses with long, easily broken legs in this landscape? Sleipnir was small for an Iceland pony. Snorre patted Sleipnir and leant forward. No, he wasn't going to change his horse.

He rode in through the gate of Reykholt at full gallop. No one was about. The inside of his thighs were stiff, and there was a thudding at his temples. His face was red with agitation. The shadows flew before him across the earth, before the whirlwind that encompassed Sleipnir and him. The sun in the west hung heavy and red amongst the strips of cloud. He pulled up hard in front of the pool, climbed off the horse and peered at the outbuildings behind the stave church. He was looking for his son, and in a way he was relieved not to see him.

He was so exhausted that he stumbled a few steps before he managed to come to a halt. Sleipnir lowered his head and sniffed at the water's surface. The horse was in a muck sweat. Wasn't the sway in Sleipnir's back more pronounced? He peered down at himself. Surely he wasn't that heavy? Sleipnir took a step nearer the pool and halted. Then Sleipnir did something he'd never done before. He put his right hoof into the hot water. He removed it again quickly, and stood as if the thing he'd just done had never happened.

Snorre gazed into the pool. A moth flew out of the light. He caught it and pressed it between his thumb and forefinger. Dust was all that was left. A cow bellowed. Sleipnir stood still. Snorre tried to look straight ahead without seeming anxious.

The decision to kill Snorre was taken after careful consideration. The way it was to be done was also arranged. After the tall man had told Gyda whose servant he was, rumours spread around Reykholt. Many people understood what was going to happen, but not when and where. They were afraid. The condemned man was unaware of what lay in store for him. The job of the two men who'd got into Snorre's house was to keep him under observation. And to try to scare or entice him, preferably alone, outside the ramparts. Further, they were to humiliate him by killing one of the people he held dearest. There weren't many to choose from. Snorre's actual murder was to left to others.

How many long trips on horseback would his worn, heavy body manage? Snorre turned his gaze on Sleipnir and imagined what it would be like to ride for days at a time across the realm he regarded as his own. The little pony was named after a giant of a horse, the eight-footed, mythological Sleipnir. The fleetest of all chargers, the one Odin himself rode. Snorre could have criss-crossed the whole of south-west Iceland, and the people he met would have stood with bowed heads. He owned most of it.

He often visited Oddi and its environs in the far south of Iceland, with its huge cliffs and the eternal breakers at their feet. Without doubt, the point at Dyrholaey, on the southernmost tip, was lovely, three hundred and fifty feet above the sea, a cacophony of bird life with views of the Vestmann Islands in the west and the dome of Myrdal-sjøkull in the north. But it wasn't this landscape that interested him most. No, it was inland, amongst the great glaciers, volcanoes, craters, geysers and mountains, that he loved to ride.

All around him it was autumn, but despite this he imagined the long trip he would make with Sleipnir in midsummer when the grass was green again. He wanted to see the grey and black stones and the mountains that reared over the restless ground, and through which the earth's inner springs vented as seething steam, boiling water and lava. He wanted to sit on Sleipnir's back once more and see redwings at nesting time, oystercatchers, ringed plovers and maybe glimpse a swan on one of the lakes. And even before Reykholt was completely out of sight, they'd have spotted black guillemot, starling, snipe and a lonely dunlin. They would ride up the Hvitá, past the church at Sidumuli to Barnafoss, to Surtshellir, the cave of dismal memories. No, perhaps not there.

They would ride high enough up the Reykholt valley to see the Langjøkull and Eiriksjøkull glaciers, and in the south, the glacier of Ok. They'd have to ride while the wind was in the south. When it was in the north or east, it would be keen as a knife. There are two things characteristic of this country, Jon Loptsson had always said: The wind blows constantly, and the people are descended from kings, not peasants. They would ride to Thingvellir in soft winds and by an indirect road.

Sleipnir was standing by the wooden door of the tunnel that led to the main house. How grateful Snorre had been for that tunnel in the winter! Duing the worst snowstorms he could walk naked from the house to the pool. He kept glancing at the rotting door. He'd made it himself out of driftwood. Could Orækja be hiding behind it? He shook his head. There had to be a limit to apprehension.

No, he decided, he would only ride when the winds were mild and there was no rain in the sky. He would ride across plains of lava and deserts of ash and around volcanoes. He'd keep well away from Hekla. The old volcano wasn't extinct. Several of the farms that had been buried in lava and ash, more than a hundred and thirty years before, had never been found. It would be better to ride to Gullfoss, the double waterfall, named for a sunny day. There, where the silver-grey Hvitá thundered over the rocks sending clouds of spray into the wind, a rainbow shone above the falls. Then they would turn and ride towards Borg, to his and Egil Skallagrimsson's old farm.

They would ride due south-west over the whole of the Reykjanes Peninsula to Bessastadir, through huge rocks from the eruptions whose hellish fire had opened the ground and swallowed more than a hundred head of his cattle. He wanted to see Grindavik and the sea beyond, where fishermen had to fight the seagulls to land their catch. Then they would head northwards, until they got to Hvalfjord, where whale skeletons littered the beach right at the top of the fjord, and the Glymur cascaded down the mountainside. They would climb by the side of the river as they stared at Esja's red peak with its flat, truncated summit.

As a young child, he'd heard the legend of the whale that had killed all the sons of Hvalfjord's priest. It swept them overboard with its great tail while they were out fishing. The next morning, the priest went down to the beach and began playing a whistle. Soon, the whale appeared. The tune made it swim in a circle, faster and faster. Playing the whole time, the priest walked towards the Glymur, and the whale followed. He went on up the waterfall and moved quickly into the mountains, the whale still following. Right at the top, and completely exhausted, the whale went pop and burst and fell down into the place that's now called Hvalfjord. Snorre never tired of this legend. Was it because he liked hearing how good had triumphed? No, he wasn't that silly. He didn't know why. Perhaps it was the thought of a whale swimming up a waterfall.

On their way to Skålholt they'd go to Faxifoss, with Hekla in the background. It wasn't the biggest waterfall he knew, but it was the most beautiful. It resembled a man in a wind.

How far would they get before he was reminded of Orækja? A mountain top, a boulder or some moss on a large stone would, sooner or later, make him compare the lines of nature with those of his son. Orækja could even ruin the landscape.

Snorre's legs no longer shook. His calves felt even more swollen than usual. Recently, this had begun to happen after any time he spent on horseback. Snorre remained where he was. Sleipnir was his most trusting subject. The horse was small enough to mount easily and without help. Tireless, obedient and, with his thick coat, irresistible company even on winter days. He could talk to Sleipnir about everything. Everything he'd wanted to say to his children, he'd told Sleipnir. He'd spoken to Sleipnir in tones that were loud, low, tender, husky or gentle, and the horse had laid his ears back attentively.

How many times had he tried to explain to his children that the seven ruling clans were treacherous? This was particularly true of the stumpy Svinfellings who owned everything from the north to the south-east. The Oddaverjes,

too, sauntering about with their crooked noses and pro-
prietorship of the areas due south and west of Vatnajøkull.
One could always try to keep in with these two clans but
the Seldøls, Vatnsfirdings, Åsbirnings and Haukdøls in the
south-west were murderous. The one thing all these clans
had in common was that they possessed weak chins and
big mouths. In addition, the Vatnsfirdings were so miserly
that they diluted their ale with horse piss.

What if Gissur, chieftain of the Haukdøls, and Kolbeinn, chieftain of the Åsbirnings, had united! It wasn't
for nothing that he'd married them both into his family.
The other clans were obsessed with grabbing the areas the
Sturlungs owned: western Iceland, parts of the Westfjords
in the north-west, most of Nordvestland and the central
part of Nordland. His children must understand this. Even
amongst the Sturlungs, greed was rife. His children often
told him he was exaggerating. Then he would reply that
their own clan might appear harmless, but they had to be
on their guard against the schemers and their lackeys. The
whole of Iceland was permeated by invisible craters into
which any careless person might fall. Orækja was the only
one of his children who listened to him. But then, Orækja
didn't understand a thing!

And what did his children know about the accumula-
tion of church property, which had begun immediately
after the establishment of the see of Skålholt in 1056? Less
than two hundred years ago. Explaining that this was crucial
to their own times made about as much impact as if he'd
been speaking to the beasts in the field. From that time
on, churches were built all over the country by the same
clans that had previously built the places of worship and
the estates. The former owners of temples and land were
now the owners of churches and land. The introduction

of tithes had made the seven clans much richer than anyone else. They held almost all the power, just like the feudal lords who ruled large regions in other parts of Europe.

Perhaps his children would sink into the peasantry. Was that what they wanted? Or would they end up as itinerants and landless people? Would they be imprisoned or killed in the depths of Surtshellir's darkness, as had happened to many others? Would they pay the tithe, or receive it? They had never shown him any gratitude for arranging wealthy marriages with the other ruling families. Apart from Orækja. But he was quite a different case.

He patted Sleipnir's back. How many times had his own children sent him reproachful looks? None of his children, or any others for that matter, perceived Sleipnir's greatness. They thought the name Snorre had given him was merely a strange whim, something one expected of a saga writer who gave Nikolas Sigurdsson, as he was being vanquished by his enemies in Norway's civil war, the line 'My escutcheon now forswears itself to me.'

The journey would culminate with a ride around the lake of Thingvallavatn and end at Thingvellir, where the Althing assembled and where he'd met Margrete for the first time. Right there, in that narrow cleft between the cliffs which has Iceland's finest echo, where he'd had his crowning moment as lawspeaker. There, he would bellow out his joy at having once more traversed the country he loved, and would never leave again.

Sleipnir lowered his head, his muzzle brushed the wet stones around the pool. Snorre carefully stroked the horse's nose without looking at it.

He glanced towards the toolstore. He couldn't see anything suspicious.

A rider came galloping from the north. He dug his feet into the sides of his horse, which couldn't move any faster. He could see the ramparts around Reykholt immediately in front of him. He had helped to build it. Earth, rocks and driftwood logs had gone into it. The north gate was open. He was looking forward to seeing his father. Orækja wanted to visit his father and find out how he was keeping. He was keen to explain the excitement of falconry. He would store his catch in the empty basket behind him.

Some miles away, Margrete went to the stable to check that the three horses she was to take to Reykholt next morning really were there. She could see Snorre's large eyes. She had said that they were mournful and beautiful.

The Norwegian king was at Nidaros, inspecting the construction of Christ's Church. To his retinue of three, he said again that Snorre had deceived him once too often, and that he was eagerly awaiting news from Iceland.

It wasn't difficult to hear that a horse was drawing near. Snorre took his eyes off the toolstore. His arms and legs were paralysed. Snorre's face was filled with fear.

'Father, I was just passing,' Orækja said.

'I've been thinking about you,' Snorre answered in a low voice.

'That's considerate,' Orækja remarked gratefully. He drew breath. 'Would it be all right if I stayed here a few days?'

'Why have you come?'

'I'm hawking.'

'Have you been here in the past few days without my knowledge?'

'I'm not usually so invisible.'

He attempted a smile. When he saw his father's deadpan face, he became serious.

'You'd have known if I was in the vicinity. At least, that's what you've always said.'

'You've never been hawking before. It's not something for a man of your rank.'

'Arnbjørg thinks it's good for me. She says that I ought to keep as far away from people as possible. D'you know what a hunting falcon fetches? There's a lot of interest in our falcons in Paris and Rome and London.'

'I'd rather you left Reykholt.'

Snorre's eyes were fixed on the ground as he spoke these words. He took a few steps towards Sleipnir and patted his back, turned and looked at his son. Orækja was taller and much leaner and stronger than him. In his belt he carried an axe and a sword. His hair was shoulder-length and his eyes blue-grey above his high cheekbones. When his son tried to speak, he cleared his throat repeatedly and stroked the bridge of his nose with his middle fingers. His father noticed that he'd got rid of his beard.

'You've never denied that I'm your son.'

Orækja looked straight at his father. Snorre averted his eyes.

'You remember the last time we met, Father, at Tumi's house at Saudafjell—you and me and Sturla. Surely you rejoice to have nephews like Tumi and Sturla?'

Snorre brushed the hair from his brow and gazed at his son. Orækja waited for his father to say something. But he didn't.

'Didn't you enjoy yourself too, Father? The food and drink were good.'

'That was when we were discussing the letter from Kolbeinn,' Snorre said quietly.

'And you reproached me for being a gullible fool. Have you ever been satisfied with me? You said that I was duped because Kolbeinn is Arnbjørg's brother. But it was you who planned the marriage.'

Snorre had never heard his son express himself so directly and clearly. He glanced over at some smooth-worn tree trunks, driftwood Kyrre had brought from Bessastadir. Should he call for help? Was it likely anyone would come? What would he do if Orækja raised his sword against him? Snorre was silent. His son observed him for signs that he wanted to say something.

Orækja turned his horse and rode back the way he'd come. His eyes were wet. Snorre shrugged his shoulders. He stood still. He looked in his son's direction and shouted after him. It was too late. Snorre felt how his heart was hammering. What had he done? He'd told Orækja to get out. His own son, the man most able to defend the estate! The old man raised his two arms skywards, like two masts waiting in vain for a sail.

A few days later Orækja wept over his father's corpse. He asked the people at Reykholt why no one had protected Snorre, and bemoaned such an injustice happening to his father, a man who'd never stuck a dagger or a sword into a living soul.

Snorre stood trembling. He'd begun to wonder who'd sent his son. He drew back his right foot and kicked a stone that lay in the grass into the water. The sun went down and took with it something of himself, something he couldn't quite put his finger on.

Snorre led Sleipnir to his stable. Then he went indoors. In front of the hearth with its dancing flames, he pulled on his nightshirt.

This was the last time father and son saw each other.

19 SEPTEMBER
1241

It was impossible to find the tiniest hint of worry in Snorre's face. No person alive could have discerned so much as a trace, or even a single line or spot of pain in the large face. He rubbed his cheeks and forehead. He'd slept well. He had made his mind up. This was to be his and Margrete's day. No one should be allowed to disturb it. He sat up in bed, blinked a couple of times to assure himself that he really was awake, glanced outside and smiled at the thought of what lay in store. Far away, the clouds vanished with the night.

Many are humbled by the passing years. The longer they live, the less significant they think their lives are. He wasn't one of them.

On the fourth-to-last day of his life, Snorre was to experience that loveliest of all forms of self-importance. He called it love. Only now, at the end of his life, was he willing to embark upon such folly. He had used up most of his time on his enemies.

After they'd met a few times, he realized that he liked her. More than that. He said that she was beautiful and that she seemed wise. He said it as awkwardly as that. She, for her part, took his words and clothed herself in them like some finely embroidered gown. He was careful to be realistic and use words he could justify. She always asked if they were true. When he repeated the things she'd already heard, she put her arms about his neck, tilted her head back and laughed in a transport of delight. Her neckline and tight-fitting waist set off her figure. And she attracted the greedy gaze of other men, too.

That oval face, those large green eyes, that straight nose and the thin lips held a discernible sorrow. It was precisely because she'd had experience of loving men that she could fix them with such an expressive look. The mere sight of a grown man was enough to excite Margrete. Not that she was frivolous, but the sight of a man gave her a tingling excitement she couldn't explain. She became a prey to passion. Often, it began as sympathy for the older and once so powerful man in his case, before becoming a series of forbidden secrets and, finally, a complex interplay between sin and the pangs of conscience. In the conflict of rapture and tears, truthfulness and growing regret, a mounting sorrow was beginning to grip her. She thought of her husband, Egil Halsteinson, and their children. When she felt at her most helpless, she abounded with virtuous attitudes. It lent her a special radiance in Snorre's eyes. Each time Margrete tried to talk to Snorre about her problems with that sly and introverted farmer, Egil, he would say that they must spend their time on each other, and not waste it on him.

Snorre had laid out his best clothes on the stool by his bed. It was almost two months since he'd taken the trouble to look well dressed. That had been for Hallveig's funeral. But now he wanted to dress for a party, for love, gaiety and seduction. It was six years since Margrete had first entered his head, only to take up residence there and furnish every corner of it. He loved her and he wasn't ashamed of it. Hallveig had known about it. At times Egil was spiteful to Snorre. However, the idea of divorcing Margrete or hurting her was unthinkable—Egil loved her too sincerely and deeply for that. The mere notion that she might not be with him, in all the ways usually reserved to man and wife, gave him a numb and panic-stricken feeling. No. Egil let Margrete meet Snorre. As long as their liaison wasn't common knowledge, he let it happen. After all, he was the one who saw most of Margrete.

Her family despised Snorre and every other Sturlung. As far as Snorre was concerned, one affair more or less wouldn't make any difference to his already frayed reputation. But his relationship with Margrete brought him anxieties that he'd never experienced before.

Snorre rubbed the sleep out of his eyes. The sun was already up. It wasn't the weather that had made him smile. Today she would come at last. Margrete had been doubtful about meeting so soon after Hallveig's death. Most of the inhabitants of Reykholt had loved Hallveig. When Margrete objected that the people of Reykholt might find her coming repugnant, he had thrown his arms around her and said that she shouldn't worry about that. He owned the estate after all. He had to see Margrete. He couldn't leave the estate, as he was frightened Oræjka would come and disrupt everything. No, he had to be on the premises. Margrete must realize that. At last, she'd promised to come.

He stood by his bed and pulled on a pair of elegant black linen breeches. Then he stooped to pick up his shirt which was on the stool. He hadn't worn it before. It was of carded white linen and he'd bought it from a merchant in southern Sweden. The breeches had been made on the estate. They fitted perfectly. The buckle on his leather belt was silver. The breeches had only been worn a few times. Normally he'd have dressed in a tunic, but not today. This was the day for his best shirt. He pulled the shirt carefully over his head. A button shone at the neck. He turned towards the door. A vivid, brownish-yellow light was reflected off the button and made him squint. Originally, there had been a pearl at the neck but he'd had it replaced with a piece of amber instead. The sleeves of the shirt were wide and had red edging on the cuffs.

Although he had lain peacefully and slept well and heavily the whole night, his hair was anything but tidy. But he was content with the trimming he'd given his beard and hair the evening before. The breeches, the shoes with laces at the ankles, the shirt, the belt and the superb button were more than enough to proclaim him well dressed. Perhaps they were even a little too much. Was it so strange that he wanted to wear his best when the sky was blue and the sailing clouds newly washed? He had experienced the deepest of all mysteries—that he could be loved.

His cloak still lay over the stool. He lifted it and inspected it thoroughly, turning it this way and that, to satisfy himself it was still just as smart. It had been packed away. The cloak was of coarse wool, red and splendid. It had three embroidered gold lines in a wavy pattern down the back. Carefully, he wound the cloak about him before fastening it with a clasp on the right side, which left his sword arm free. The clasp, with its three gold heads, held the cloak together. He reached behind him and straightened it. Now there was only one thing lacking. Wouldn't that wide-brimmed leather hat of his complete the picture? But first he mustn't forget the gold bracelet. He'd hidden it under his pillow. Was that why he'd slept so well last night? When the lord of Reykholt wanted to dress up, he always wore this bracelet on his right arm. He put it on quickly. The bracelet's motif was a snake biting its own tail. He combed his hair slowly, and then carefully tended his beard. His hair had turned greyer over the past year.

Hallveig had given him the hat. He could tell Margrete he'd got it in Norway. Hallveig had bought it from a merchant in Bremen. Until that moment he'd never had it on his head. When Hallveig asked why he wouldn't wear the hat, he'd said it was too nice. Men in Iceland didn't wear hats. He was no show-off. Today he did try the hat, looking at himself in the copper cauldron on the long table. He bent his knees and sat on his haunches in front of the cauldron. Using both hands he tried the hat at various angles and positions on his large head. He stood up, paced to and fro a number of times, squatted down again, gazed at his reflection, made a slight adjustment, rose and strode the floor before staring into the cauldron one more time. Suddenly, he threw the hat on the floor and shouted: 'Never!'

After a while he returned to the dented hat. He picked it up, straightened it and placed the hat gingerly on his head. Without looking into the cauldron, he positioned himself in the middle of the room. He pondered for a while. He felt the weight of the hat, talked earnestly to himself, made small gestures and pointed to his head. His face was mild, friendly and candid. After a while, a few disjointed words emerged. Snorre rehearsed every single line before receiving his love in his own home.

At thirty-one, Margrete was half his age. Her long blonde hair, her big green eyes beneath the dark brows, her freckles, the tiny scar under her lower lip, even her laughter, her voice, reminded him not a little of another woman he'd thought he loved—Orækja's mother. Snorre never mentioned this striking resemblance to Margrete. It wasn't just a matter of looks but also of temperament. He had kept both relationships secret. Snorre knew that they could prove inopportune.

He paced between bed, hearth, stool, long table, door, window, guest's bed, Hallveig's loom and the little cupboard where he kept a supply of bread and milk. That was all he felt like eating. It had been two days since Gyda had brought him hot food. He'd told her he didn't want to be disturbed, she'd curtsied and made to leave. But on the way out, she'd surprised herself by asking if he was going to write, as she'd spotted the quill on the table. He pretended not to understand the question and waved her away.

Snorre walked calmly amongst the objects in the spacious room. He talked to himself. Not loudly or with any grand gestures, but quietly. He weighed each sound even as it remained lying on his tongue. The short, tranquil steps had neither pattern nor plan. Each time he neared an object, he gave it a wide berth. Occasionally, he'd grasp the long table with his right hand, doff his hat with the left and mumble smilingly out into the room. Then, all at once, his aimless wandering ceased. He stood erect, with his arms by his sides. In a clear voice, he asked himself if he oughtn't to go outside.

'It's a fine day out there. But that's not everything. Perhaps my clothes look better indoors? No, on the contrary, outdoors is where they really show to advantage.'

He gazed across the yard. Could nobody chase those sheep away? Would they lift a finger if the sheep found where the winter fodder was stored? What remained of fresh grass would soon be consumed. All those sheep he'd once had. All that money he'd made selling homespun cloth to Norway and the Continent. After they began dyeing wool in France and Holland, he'd had to reduce the size of his flocks. More and more cattle had filled the landscape around Reykholt.

'I can't go out in these clothes. It's impossible.'

Perhaps he should go out anyway? Wouldn't it look odd? Odd? Mad! On the other hand, it would show Margrete much-deserved respect. Great respect!

His eyes assumed a doubtful expression. His arms still hung limp, and then his right arm raised itself slowly, and brought his hand hesitantly to his head. His middle finger just touching the hat.

'What if she doesn't turn up!'

For the second time he tore the hat off, hurled it to the ground and kicked it under the bed.

Snorre had never met a more generous woman than Margrete. She was unconcerned about the gossip over his former affair with Solveig. He was no less taken with her. Maybe Margrete really loved him? Solveig and Snorre were more than good friends, even after he married Hallveig. It was Solveig's inheritance from her father that had brought them together. Solveig's father, Sæmundr Jonsson of Oddi, had remained unmarried all his life, but he'd had five children all the same. Shortly before he died, he decided that his daughter should inherit an equal portion with each of his four sons. It was decided that Snorre should oversee the settlement. Snorre fetched Solveig from her mother at Keldur. He had a large retinue with him. Solveig was beautiful. Snorre informed Solveig's mother that she didn't need to accompany them to Oddi, where the settlement was to take place. He would ensure that Solveig returned safely with her ample share of the inheritance and perhaps something more besides.

Snorre rode ahead with Solveig. He told the others to ride a couple of horses' lengths behind. They conversed easily. It wasn't that they didn't occasionally disagree on the road from Keldur to Oddi, but each time it was defused by laughter and the pleasure of knowing how well they understood each other. Their glances met in quick smiles. This pleased them both.

After half a day's travel, Snorre and Solveig spied a woman riding towards them. The woman was accompanied by one man. Some distance away, Snorre and Solveig began to ask each other with some considerable amusement, what the woman could possibly be wearing on her head. Just as the horses drew level, they saw what it was. The woman had taken the corners of her cloak and tied them over her head. Without the least smile or comment, she rode between Snorre and Solveig. She didn't even nod. Snorre said loudly: 'A very good day to you.'

Solveig said nothing until the woman had passed. She knew quite well who she was. Snorre and Solveig turned. They regarded the woman and her silent escort, who didn't look around, but rode majestically on. The escort was a man of almost eighty, riding erect on his horse. Solveig began to giggle. 'Ridiculous,' said Snorre before they both shared the joke.

The woman who'd passed them had a face that was neither ugly nor pretty. She was the widow of Bjørn Thorvaldsson and Iceland's richest woman, Hallveig Ormsdottir. Some years later, Snorre courted her. Hallveig's position and wealth aroused stronger emotions in him than Solveig could command. Although Snorre was attracted to Solveig, it was nothing compared to what he felt for Margrete. It was an obsession he would never lose. She was the only one who was capable of affecting him so that he felt he could, for an instant, hold on to the days and years he had left.

He paced back and forth in the big room, as empty of purpose as a fly in a bottle. The thought of Margrete completely engulfed him. At each step he listened for her. She must be there soon!

Snorre's ears were of generous size, fleshy and plump, especially the lobes. His hearing was still good. He often mentioned this fact, adding, as if it were the first time he'd said it, that those who wanted to speak ill of him would have to whisper so softly that only a fly could hear them. Wasn't that her now?

He gave his cloak and breeches a quick brush with his hands to make sure that everything was as it should be, and touched the amber button once again before hastening to the door. It must be her. His calfskin shoes had slippery soles, but the feet were placed with decisiveness. He was nowhere near falling. His weight was on his left leg. His thigh was fully tensed. He gave it no thought. With his right hand, he threw open the door. The smell of grass hit him. The air wasn't warm but it was pleasant. Dressed in his best, he held the door handle in his right hand, raising his left, fingers outstretched, in a greeting. The horse reared, whinnied, stamped its forelegs on the ground, shook its mane, showed its teeth, raised and lowered its head and staring eyes. He searched frantically for the rider. Where was she? He took two paces forward. Had she fallen off?

The horse was chestnut with white patches. It reared again. Its quivering back legs were strong. The horse raised its hooves in his direction. He sidestepped. His eyes sought along the wall of the house. The horse raised itself for the third time. Had she fallen off it? He stepped outside. He shouted her name. The horse neighed. Otherwise all was silent. He didn't recognize the horse. Why was it frightened? He soothed it. It trotted in a circle, whinnied and disappeared. Why hadn't anyone come out of the houses to take care of the horse? He called her name again. He glanced down at his clothes. What was he doing? He looked about. Still no one in sight. He went back to the open door. He closed it quickly behind him. He raised his feet, stamped on the floor, cursed and swore. After a few minutes he seated himself on the long bench.

That he could be loved by a woman like Margrete seemed unimaginable. His agreement with Hallveig had only been financial at first. It had benefitted them both. After a while, they'd begun to respect one another. But love? No.

After Margrete had made her feelings for him clear, he'd reminded her that she was married. She asked him if he could conceive how many times she'd reminded herself of exactly the same thing during the past months. Contemptibly enough, he'd asked if it was his money, power or property that interested her. She hadn't lowered her eyes or begun to cry, but brushed the hair away from her eyes and said that she had sufficient goods and wealth. She loved him! He stood there. He didn't touch her.

Eventually he said he couldn't believe it. Could she really be in love with a man of his age and appearance? He mentioned his corpulent head, his bent nose, the weak chin one anticipated beneath the beard, his over-large body, his fat fingers which appeared all the more strange on his slender hands, his incipient shiny pate, his unkempt hair, even his slow mode of speech—could she seriously be attracted by all this? She was silent while he spoke. She looked at him. He was sincere. Yes, indeed he was. Still she said nothing. Was he afraid of her infatuation? Because he knew he would never be capable of returning it? He became even more voluble and reminded her he was an elderly man, that he was becoming wrinkled, that he despised and detested his old age. Only when she took a breath so deep that it was audible did he stop. Her eyes were still on his. He told her he talked too much, and now he'd added that, too. She looked down and smiled before heaven opened. She raised her dark lashes, her eyelids and her green eyes, and met his glance.

She said that one of the first things to arouse her interest had been the way he used words, and yes, his knowledge too, perhaps.

He turned and indicated that he had other things to do. Over the next few days, he began to wonder why he couldn't get Margrete out of his head.

The next time Snorre met Margrete, it was general knowledge that he'd entered into a major business arrangement with Gunnar Haldorsson. She told him that he ought to withdraw from it immediately. Margrete explained that she and her husband knew Gunnar to be a rogue.

'He's a swindler. The people he's tricked before are going to set fire to everything he owns within a day or two. You'll never get the cod you paid for. Ask for the return of your money! Doesn't the money mean anything to you?'

She lowered her eyes. Even now, at this meeting, he still pretended she meant nothing to him. As soon as she was out of sight, he rode to Gunnar as fast as he could and got the money back. Gunnar wanted to know Snorre's reasons for rescinding the agreement they'd drunk to. He wasn't too dear, surely? Snorre shook his head. He'd changed his mind. Was that because he'd asked for the money in advance? No, it was simply that he didn't need the cod any more. Snorre tried to sound as convincing as possible.

That evening, Gunnar's house and business were completely destroyed in a fire. What happened that night was just what the ambitious merchant had feared most of all. He had himself witnessed a great fire amongst the fishing businesses at Vågan in Lofoten the previous year. The following day, Snorre examined the site of the fire. Gunnar's charred remains were not difficult to spot amongst the smoke. His blackened right hand was clenched. Those Snorre spoke to thought he'd been hammering on the door in a vain attempt to escape. Snorre waited until late in the afternoon before riding home. He became pensive. He wandered down to the seashore. He took off his shoes, waded out into the cold water and saw the waves receding from the beach, the sea grasping at the coast's retreating line, the water sinking into the sand leaving the imprint of age and loss. Where was the sea going?

'To her lover,' he muttered.

Next time he met Margrete at the Althing, he asked her how she'd known what was going to happen to Gunnar Haldorsson. He asked if she knew the people who'd set the fire. Was he saying she was in league with the arsonist? She began to cry. They each sat on their own horses. As soon as Snorre saw her tears, he got off Sleipnir, went over to her and begged her forgiveness. He wanted so much to stroke her cheek. He had to content himself with brushing his hand across the lower part of her dress and patting her horse. He glanced by turns at her and her husband—he stood a little way off. Although he'd really finished his business at the Althing, he stayed another day to get the opportunity of comforting her again. Away from her husband's eyes, he embraced her, caressed every bit of her bare skin and kissed her. She let him do it.

He went to the feasting hall and back again. The sun was past its zenith. Margrete should have been here by now. He looked out. He couldn't see anyone. He opened the door. All was quiet. He went down on his haunches to see if he could hear the sound of galloping hooves. Could something have happened to her? He ran outside. He didn't care that there were others at Reykholt who might be staring at him. He was dressed as if for his own wedding. Ready to meet his love. He didn't care what his family or the others on the estate might say. He wanted *her*. No one else.

'Margrete!' Where was she? Something had happened. Nothing must get in their way. He had to have her there with him, even if it was for the last time. He clenched his fists until his knuckles turned white. His arms were straight. The clenched fists trembled. The nails dug into his palms. A tingling spread from his fists up to his elbows. He shouted out her name. He looked around. He didn't care if people were gazing in his direction. He had only one thought, that his shouts might conjure up her beautiful presence, sitting on a horse, riding towards him. Nothing happened. Wasn't she coming after all? Had her husband prevented her?

If, with a whole world of words, he'd been able to explain how and why he loved her, he wouldn't have loved her. If he'd been offered a fortune there and then, it would have been as nothing compared to her standing there, large as life. Nothing could replace her. Everything else was grey by comparison. He'd never experienced such a feeling before. Greed, pride and all his ambitions united in one desire—that he might see her again.

Once, she'd asked if he was jealous. He assumed the question related to that painful episode with Knut Storskald. He'd tried to be honest and said that Knut was a handsome man with fine curls, and that this had made him envious. She'd asked if his envy wasn't more because he'd stopped writing poetry whereas Knut had continued. This wasn't so wide of the mark, but he shook his head. He'd drunk too much at the Althing the previous year. Snorre and Margrete had been standing talking to Knut in the marketplace. Knut had conveyed greetings to Snorre from his kinsman Duke Skúli. Margrete had praised Knut for the poems he'd read earlier that day.

Luck must exist, or it would be impossible to explain enmity's successes.

Margrete's gaze shifted to two farmers who were haggling over the price of a couple of cows. One word capped the next, cursing and swearing rent the air. Snorre's gaze was fixed rigidly on Knut. Knut pulled a face at him and began to copy Snorre's way of walking, that heavy, somewhat clumsy and hesitant gait. Then, an event occurred which Snorre found impossible to explain adequately. He took a couple of quick steps and kicked Knut, who let out a howl and fell to the ground, clutching his upper thigh.

'What have you done?' Margrete shouted.

'He was making a fool of me,' he answered submissively. She shook her head and turned away, clearly embarrassed, before going over to Knut, helping him to his feet and begging his pardon. He felt a tingling in his cheek. The popinjay had the audacity to stare at him, shamelessly, and as if that wasn't enough, he was smiling as well.

This time Snorre kicked harder. What he hadn't considered was that the power in his right leg and foot had eclipsed the strength and balance of his left. Suddenly, and without sufficient warning, his left leg was subjected to a strain it hadn't known for many years. The young poet jumped out of the way, and Snorre fell heavily. He fell awkwardly, with the dust swirling up around him. Margrete turned and looked first at Snorre and then at Knut. She was laughing at him! That evening Snorre told Margrete at least ten times that she'd been laughing.

If only she'd arrive! Perhaps something had happened to the children? If that were the case, she would never leave them. He knew that. What would he have done himself? He would have chosen his love. If she truly loved him, she wouldn't shrink from any effort or pain to keep her appointment. No other duties, people or threats would be allowed to get in the way.

He repeated her name to himself. He loved her because she was everything he was not. She had firm opinions. He'd always weigh up the pros and cons until it was too late. At the same time he wanted to have and to own everything. Her determination reminded him of his daughter, Thordis, whose eyes were so blue that you thought you were talking to the sky. If only Margrete would come riding across the yard. All that mattered was her and him. If only he could see her. Even if only for a moment, he would treasure it as his dearest and fondest memory.

The clouds drifted eastwards across the sky.

A flock of birds appeared from nowhere. What sort they were was of no consequence to him. But the noise of the birds was impossible to ignore. Fish entrails had been thrown from a window. For a few seconds they circled the swollen guts, then dived on their prey. They pecked at each other's heads to form a queue. The last, a young bird, had to content itself with the bones and the scraps of skin that lay untouched.

His clothes no longer interested him. He had called out the only name that mattered to him. He was numbed by the idea that she might be dead. He walked to the nearest mound, weeping as he spoke.

'She's dead. Of course she's dead.'

There was silence for a moment. He gasped for breath. He sank down on all fours and drooped his head. He sobbed. He was on his hands and knees in his best clothes. His tears mingled with the dust. No one at Reykholt had ever seen him like this. Even as a child at Oddi he hadn't behaved in this fashion. Just as he was about to draw breath, he felt it. First in his fingers and then his knees. The faint vibration of hooves. There was no mistake. They were approaching. Was it a lone horse? No, there must be several, but not many. He got up hastily, wiped his tears away with his hand and quickly dusted off his breeches.

'It must be her,' he muttered as he trotted up and down the yard. 'I knew she'd come. Of course I could trust her. How could I ever doubt it? What was I thinking?'

He never considered fetching his sword, or trying to gather the Reykholt men who were able to bear arms. The idea never occurred to him. Now, four days before his life was to end, he thought that horses nearing the estate could only be bringing good news. He kept repeating it was her several times, as if to assure himself even more. He stood in the middle of the yard, adjusting his clothes yet again, running his fingers through his beard and repeating some of the lines he'd rehearsed to himself.

The white hen which had been flitting about in front of the house over the past few days stood before the door. She ruffled her feathers, tapped on the closed door with her beak and stretched her neck towards the window. The door wasn't opened. She tapped the door even harder. Nothing happened. After a while she tripped off uncertainly. Then she approached a bowl at the corner of the house, filled with rainwater from the last shower. Here, she rolled, beat her wings wildly and shook off the night's fleas. Far away, lightning sent a tongue of fire against a lonely tree.

The horses were approaching fast. They were coming from an unusual direction. Surely they should make their appearance soon? Why didn't Kyrre or the servant girl or any of the others come out to see who it was? Everyone could hear that there were people arriving. Snorre wanted everyone to see her. He was so proud of her! There was no reason to hide away now. It was the moment before the arrival. He stood in the middle of the yard. He stood on tiptoe. There, he caught a glimpse of them. Were there really only two horses? A chestnut and a black. Wasn't anyone riding them? They galloped wildly into the yard. There she was. Margrete, riding in front on the chestnut. He held out his arms. She was holding the other horse's reins.

'Are you alone?'

He stared at her—the green eyes, the thin lips, the long, light hair tied in a violet silk ribbon. She hadn't altered. She was the same.

'I've lost the other horse,' she said breathlessly. 'It's chestnut with white patches. It broke loose and ran ahead. Have you seen it?'

He saw the pupils surrounded by dark green. The cheekbones, the mouth, the throat.

'Yes,' he nodded. 'Kyrre will have tethered it next to the other horses.'

He pointed towards the stable.

She gave a smile of relief and took a breath.

'How are you?'

'I'm happy because I'm able to come to you. It is beautiful here at Reykholt,' she said as calmly as she could.

Her face was warm and cheerful, her features exuded joy at seeing the large, ageing man with his slightly stooping form. But even so, her face occasionally assumed an uneasy air. She gazed about her. Reykholt was exactly as she'd imgined it. She asked where the pool was. He pointed. He asked why she'd brought three horses along. She explained that she needed a fresh horse on hand the whole time to get along fast enough. She said he must take care of himself. She embraced him. Of course he'd take care. She held him gently away from her. She looked at him. She smiled. She said she'd never seen him so smart. She made special mention of the amber button and his elegant clasp. And his beard? Had he really trimmed it? He nodded. She laughed. He put his arm round her shoulder.

He looked at the long hair that fell loose from a bun at her neck. She wore a grey linen shift under an azure woollen dress. The dress had shoulder straps, fastened by a couple of cup-shaped gold clasps. She'd had a red cloak across her shoulders which she'd removed as she rode into the yard. Around her neck was a chain of rock-crystal pearls mounted in silver. He thought they were beautiful.

'You sparkle,' he said. She ran her hand across the pearls and looked up at him, smiled and nodded. Yes, she agreed. She'd been given them by a merchant from Gotland who wanted to seal an important bargain with her husband. He put his arm round her shoulder and steered her towards the door. She glanced left and right. On the threshold, she turned. Were they alone? Just as she was about to go in, she remembered that she needed the two bags on the black horse's back. Snorre had hitched the horses to the wooden rail outside. He immediately offered to carry the bags. She handed them to him, thanked him, pushed the hair away from her brow and went indoors. They were heavier than he'd expected. Without asking, he opened them. As soon as he opened the larger one, a wonderful smell assailed his nostrils. Had she known? Had he let it slip at one time or another? It was the most heavenly of all smells. His nose tried to catch the blissful aromas that came from the soapstone pot. He was sure she'd brought mutton stew in the pot. He didn't ask to find out, but to make the conversation flow more easily. She nodded. She said he'd let drop that mutton stew was his favourite. Not just once but three times. Had he really done that? He laughed. She laughed in return. But the idea hadn't been for her to prepare the food. Surely she knew he had servants for that?

'We may feel we want to be alone,' she said. Her face was serious. He saw her expression. She noticed him looking at her. She took the pot from him and carried it over to the long hearth. She hooked the pot to the chain that hung down from the roof beam. He lit the fire. He asked where he should put the bags. He didn't ask why she'd packed two daggers in the second one. From the small cupboard next to the bed, Snorre got out two silver cups and a jug of cherry wine. Or would she prefer proper red wine from the Rhine valley? He knelt down, peering into the cupboard. He asked again if he shouldn't ask the servants to prepare the banquet she deserved. Wasn't the mutton stew good enough? It would soon be hot, she said. Of course! He hadn't meant it like that. He had bread in the cupboard. He opened his arms and apologized for his thoughtlessness.

'Do you want fruit wine as well as red wine?' She made no answer. He took out both. He placed the cups on the long table, with a loaf of bread, a knife and a silver spoon for each of them. He had plenty of beer as well, but perhaps they could leave that for later? She nodded and asked who the big loom had belonged to. She glanced at the weaving that Hallveig had left unfinished. Margrete nodded appreciatively and muttered something about twill weaves. He didn't understand a word she said. He nodded. He looked at her.

Margrete was no longer breathless. He went up to her. Snorre lowered his own head closer to hers. He felt the warmth of her forehead. He tried to kiss her. She turned away.

He poured out the fruit wine. They toasted one another. Snorre asked if there'd been any problems on the way over. She shook her head. She knew which road to take. He didn't understand what she meant. Had anything else of note happened? He tried to put his arms around her. She hesitated a little. He reached for her arm.

Yes, of course there had been something. She'd seen a swan, she said. A big, well-nourished swan. It had glided round the still lake, like a sleigh, from cloud to cloud. It was so hungry for the clouds that were constantly forming.

She glanced at Snorre's marvelling eyes. She looked at the loom, before settling her gaze back on him once more.

He said nothing. He was surprised how his thoughts suddenly turned to his wife Hallveig after disease had ravaged her for many years. From now on, she'd told him in Gyda's presence, he'd have to go to other women. The mistress of Reykholt was no whore. Gyda had nodded and curtsied.

Snorre had told Margrete about Hallveig one of the first times they met. He spoke of her with respect, as someone who in many ways was braver than he was.

Despite giving birth to two children, it was only after she'd been with Snorre the first time that Margrete began to enjoy her own body. Later the same night, she'd lain down naked under the covers with her husband snoring next to her. After some hesitation, and assuring herself that her husband really was asleep, she'd fondled her breasts before her fingers found their way between her thighs. She could hear Snorre's words the whole time, about how he'd always have her in his mind, the fantasies he had about her, his dreams about living with her. But most of all, she'd treasured his gaze, the gaze she imagined each night in the darkness of her marital bed, the one that undressed her. In the light of the following day, she'd told herself that she must get him out of her head. And each time she said it, the hot, illicit thoughts of the older man returned with greater force.

She had tried to resist! It was hopeless. With increasing regularity she began to conjure up in her mind what it would be like to strip naked before him by a small lake, safe from everyone except the moon. She would stand on the margin, the water would be black beyond the stones, he would watch her unfasten the jewellery around her neck and her bracelet, loosen the hair grip, before she'd step out of the long, red dress, showing the whole of her body as if she'd emerged from a petal, and walk carefully across the stones and into the water. It had been two years since she'd imagined the moon and the two of them for the first time.

She moved close to Snorre, put her hands on his shoulders and pulled him to her. He kissed her. She let him do it. Margrete took his hand and led him towards the bed. They kissed. He knocked a candle over, it went out. Their clothes landed in a pile. She was so lovely. He covered himself with his undershirt. She snatched it from him and threw it on the floor. She pulled him closer to her. She lay down first. She reached up her arms for him. He noticed the fair hairs on her forearms. She raised her head from the pillow, smiled and asked what he was waiting for. He shook his head, stretched out his hand for her arm and placed his knee on the bed, followed by the rest of his big body. She smoothed his chin. He kissed her unhurriedly, tilted his head and kissed her more passionately.

She was so naked. He noticed how rough his fingers were. It's tempting here to give a detailed description of how she got ready, took hold of his head and guided it between her thighs and squeezed closer to him until, moaning and gasping, she gripped him with her right hand and arm, and with her left helped to pull him harder in. Here, everyone may add or subtract, according to how much bashfulness distorts their lives. What is certain is that Margrete lifted the shaggy head, kissed it and replaced it between her thighs and thought of how many men, over the centuries, had lain on their stomachs like this, and how many women had stroked his shaggy head, then thought, of all things, of childbirth, before drawing him over and into her. Snorre remembered kissing her final thought on the brow before falling asleep.

They rose before evening. It was the last time they would get up together. She peered out at the dwarf birch, which every day was gilded by the first and last rays of the sun. He used a word he'd never used before. He said he was happy. They drank some wine. He asked why she'd suddenly gone so silent. She didn't want to answer. He noticed. He asked again. She said she was frightened for the children and about what might happen to him.

'Please, listen to what I'm saying!' she reiterated.

'Calm down, I know how to defend myself. You know that, don't you?' He put his arm around her. She laid her head against his. He stroked her hair, kissed her cheek, rose and lifted the drinking horn from the wall. It was decorated with painstakingly worked metal ornamentation around the rim. Jon Loptsson had presented it to him on his fifteenth birthday. The bull's horn was full of beer. He asked if she'd drunk beer from a horn before. She shook her head.

'Won't you try for my sake?'

She was about to ask if he hadn't understood the seriousness of what she'd said. She said she'd certainly try drinking from the horn.

'Even that's a skill you have to learn,' he said laughing. He hadn't drunk beer for many weeks. But now he did want to drink, to celebrate and be glad that she'd arrived at last. And not just that—he wanted to ask her if she'd consider moving to Reykholt. She asked to feel the weight of the drinking horn. Was she interrupting him? They had one at home too, but this one looked heavier—was that mere imagination? He passed it to her. She shook her head. Snorre explained that if she had second thoughts, she had to remember that the first trickle quickly turned into a tidal wave. Perhaps he could show her? Another problem was that it was difficult to put it down unless it was empty. He laughed. She didn't mention that he could have hung it up again after a few draughts instead. She'd never seen him so happy and light-hearted. She delighted in his boyish eagerness. She drank from the horn, made a mess and laughed with him before he took over and drained it. Just as he was about to hand it over for the second time, he stumbled and dropped it on the floor. She giggled. He laughed and wrapped his arms around her, raised her up and carried her back to the bed. They looked at one another. Love is time that stands still in the eyes.

They fell asleep with a sheepskin over them. Their clothes lay with the guttering candle and the drinking horn on the floor. Embers still glowed in the long hearth. Margrete had packed away the cooking pot in the bag that lay next to the bed. She was thinking of Egil. He was probably talking to the children about her and Snorre. He would certainly be encouraging them to hate her. Snorre was sleeping heavily. The dwarf birch outside quivered slightly. A gentle breeze had come with darkness. The branches stirred. The outermost leaves whispered to one another.

20 SEPTEMBER
1241

Margrete managed to slip out of bed without disturbing Snorre. She dressed, stood by the door and stared for a long time at the big man still lying there. He slept peacefully beneath the sheepskin. She was about to creep back and kiss his cheek, but changed her mind. She heard a breath of wind rustling the birch outside. The horses were quiet. She had to get away unnoticed before he woke up.

She opened the door carefully, it didn't creak as much as she'd feared. The horses were still asleep in the stable. She waited a moment before leading her three horses out. Then she laid the bags over the chestnut and led them away from the main house and up to the south gate. She knew that Kyrre the stable boy was following her with his eyes from where he stood hidden behind the open stable door. She mounted the chestnut, the fastest and toughest horse. After one more look back, she dug her heels into its flanks. The other horses trotted obediently behind. When the sun rose and she could feel its heat warming her cheek, she spied three riders coming towards her. Her back stiffened. Ought she to change direction? If she rode northwards, would she be able to avoid them? She decided to ride straight on. Their clothes looked unusual and they carried no obvious weapons. She was riding faster than them. They were just about to pass each other. She thought she recognized the costume of the one who rode first. He wasn't wearing the clerical garb usually seen in Iceland. The other two must be the priest's servants. As soon as they'd passed each other on the narrow cart track, Margrete turned to take in the group. There could be no doubt. She'd seen priests in Rome wearing the same tunics.

The priest's surname was Ugolino, and he was distantly related to the pope, Gregory IX. It was imperative that he find Snorre. One of his servants spoke broken Icelandic. The other servant had a leather cord around his neck attached to a cylindrical leather case. Inside was a letter from the pope written in Latin, with a copy in Icelandic. The party was on its way to Reykholt. The letter was addressed to Snorre. Both the pope and his emissaries believed he was still Iceland's most powerful man. The first paragraph of the letter was a description of a man the pope despised more than any other—Emperor Frederick II. The next was a comprehensive account of the compromise the emperor had made with the infidels in Jerusalem. Finally, the letter contained a strong request, almost an injunction, for Iceland and Norway to unite Scandinavia in a Crusade that would liberate Jerusalem.

They were taking the best-trodden road to Reykholt. All the time Margrete could see them, a cloud of dust followed a few yards behind the three.

Half asleep, Snorre reached for Margrete. He wanted to stroke her back, her hips and kiss the nape of her neck above the chain that carried the gold crucifix, the only ornament she wore under her clothes. He opened his eyes. His hand searched for her, and his mouth mumbled her name.

He was out of bed in one bound. He clutched his best breeches lying on the floor and pushed his right foot down the leg. The breeches were inside out. He gave up and threw them on the floor. His left leg was asleep. He staggered, stamped his foot on the floor until the circulation returned and he could walk normally. He ran out naked.

Her horses had gone! She'd gone off without saying good-bye. Not a sign, not a word that she was going to leave.

He invoked God's name. He asked for God's help, and then roundly abused him. Full of contrition, he begged both God and Margrete's pardon for reproaching them. Perhaps someone had spirited her away against her will? That was it, of course! Had Egil arrived during the night? Had he used the children as a threat? Snorre cursed his propensity to sleep heavily. No other footprints were visible. He knelt outside the door to check one more time. He rose and squinted across the yard. Then he summoned God's help again. His urgent prayer was directed to a God who knows no moderation. He appealed to a God who quite often loses control. After creating the beetle, not content with one species, he made three hundred thousand more. The impotent Snorre implored God's forgiveness and understanding. Breathless, he walked across the yard to ask Kyrre if he'd seen her. On this occasion, Kyrre managed to hide in time.

He went indoors as fast as he could, put on what he found on the floor, a threadbare tunic and his best breeches, which he'd turned rightside out. Hurriedly, he left the house again. He was barefoot. He must ride after her. He went to the stable. Could he hear something? He'd manage on his own, he shouted. Sleipnir wasn't there! Sleipnir was nowhere to be seen.

'Can you hear me, Kyrre?' resounded all about the yard.

Snorre peered out of the stable door. He considered a moment before walking into the yard.

He must ride after Margrete immediately. Poor woman, living on that godforsaken farm, away from the road. An ugly place fit only for one thing—drinking yourself to death unobserved. He'd told her as much. She'd looked away.

He'd have to take one of the other horses, they were all his anyway. The southern gate was open. The only thing he could see was a herd of cows with lowered heads. They were standing there to hold the sky up. Snorre clutched his heart, breathed deeply, spun round and went back to the stable as fast as he could. Which of the horses should he take? Kyrre could have advised him, but there was no time for that. Snorre moved quickly over to the largest white horse. He'd seen Kyrre ride it sometimes.

Snorre talked to the horse. It seemed to be good-tempered. He patted it. He led it out into the daylight. He carried a little hay in his left hand which he gave to the horse as soon as they were outside. Snorre spoke to the horse as he mounted. It had been many years since he'd ridden any horse other than Sleipnir. He didn't like it. He had no choice. First he put it into a slow trot, then into a running walk, before breaking into a gallop. Snorre rode around Reykholt's ramparts.

There was no sign of Margrete. The northern gate was shut. He went back to the southern one at a slow trot. He halted the horse some yards away. It stamped listlessly, and at first he couldn't understand why, but then he remembered the vein of the hot spring beneath their feet that fed the pool. He looked down at the ground. Horse and rider formed a long, mobile, slanting shadow. He hoped the spring would continue to pass Reykholt in the future. Originally it had run fifteen miles north-east of the estate. Snorre's mother had told him that the spring had moved because an innocent man had been killed and his gory clothes had been washed in the spring. The spring wanted to avenge the murdered man, and moved closer to

Reykholt. There, yet another innocent victim's clothes were washed in it. And the spring moved for the second time. This time it moved right next to the houses at Reykholt, where it remained. Snorre's mother had also said that if three consecutive priests came to Reykholt, all bearing the same Christian name, the spring would disappear. Snorre laughed at this tale, but ever since he, and every previous owner of the Reykholt estate and church fief, had paid greater attention to the applicants' first names whenever the living was vacant.

A whinny from close by caught his ear. It was Sleipnir! Who had let him loose outside the ramparts? He rode quickly over to Sleipnir, dismounted Kyrre's horse and got up on his own, then led the other back to the stable.

Orækja was a day's ride from Reykholt. Why did everything always go wrong when he met his father? He hadn't even been given a meal. How many times had Snorre told him that he ought to be repenting something or other? But it was almost invariably Snorre who'd sent him on these missions. And now he couldn't even stay the night at his childhood home. His father ought to know that things didn't always turn out the way one expected. He couldn't admit responsibility and show remorse when there was no cause to. If he made a false plea for forgiveness, his father would find him out immediately. And when he said nothing, his father was convinced he was trying to trick him. He was always in the wrong. In his father's eyes, he was always guilty. As a teenager, Orækja had opposed his father. In adulthood, he'd capitulated and tried to behave fondly towards him. His wife Arnbjørg had tried, on several occasions, to get him to argue when Snorre was being unreasonable. To no purpose. The last time his father had sent him up north to Isafjord to keep the Vatnsfirdings in check, the same thing had happened. His father thought he'd done it all wrong. He hadn't tried to negotiate with the rebels before crushing them with brute force. Why hadn't he taken the time to assess the consequences of that brutal decision?

'Next time you should come along too,' said O
ækja.

'Can't I depend on you any more?' his father parried.

'Is there a more devoted son in the whole of Iceland?'

His father didn't reply.

'You know that I'm proud of you. I couldn't have a better father.'

Snorre turned away.

There are souls which even God himself cannot save. Not even if God fell on his knees and pleaded for them.

'So you mean, Father, that I'm unworthy to sing your praises? Or . . .' and Oækja recalled that he'd hesitated before continuing, alarmed at the import of his words, 'is it because you're not certain you deserve them?'

His father remained silent. For once, he didn't know what to say.

Oækja leant forward on his horse and patted its mane. For a time, Oækja had assumed that his father was brusque because he felt guilty about his relationship with Margrete. Oækja had said it was quite all right by him, but that hadn't softened his father.

He began thinking about the journey home to Iceland with his father two years before. The voyage had begun so peacefully. He remembered that they'd both joked and laughed about King Håkon's attempts to keep them in Norway. The fact that his father was quite happy to bawl him out in front of other people was one thing. But that he'd allowed himself to be tied to that thwart on his father's orders amazed him. Still, he'd accepted it, without resistance, without one single word of abuse. The mate had glanced at him a number of times. Why wasn't he yelling imprecations at his father? Orækja recalled how the mate had by turns looked anxiously at him and his father, who was staring at the mirror-calm sea. Now and then, Orækja had allowed his eyes to rest on the others aboard. They had stared at the deck or over the gunwale as if frightened that he might go mad and knock the mate down before having a final showdown with his father and throwing him overboard. The fact that it hadn't happened, and that he'd let himself be humbled without a word of protest, had surprised them more than it did him. Orækja was right about their course, but if the men aboard had taken action it would have humiliated his father. That was the last thing Orækja wanted. It would, he had to admit, have offended him even more.

Orækja spurred his horse to a gallop. Everything he was, his position and rank, he owed to his father. His father was wise and scholarly, but he wasn't. He was a hothead, needlessly brutal, ignorant of what he could set in train. His father had said as much. How could his father have been so certain he wouldn't resist when he'd given the order to bind him fast? There hadn't been a trace of uneasiness in his father's face. Not a twitch, not even a furrow had appeared. Orækja wanted to continue hawking for a few more days. Perhaps he could ride back to Reykholt some other time.

After tethering the white horse in the stable, Snorre rode out of the south gate once more. At a distance he spied a small group riding slowly towards Reykholt. Snorre dug his heels into Sleipnir's flanks. After a few yards he changed his mind. He eased Sleipnir into a slow trot and rode in a circle. Snorre stared at the group slowly wending its way towards him. Was she amongst them? He rode up the knoll. No, she wasn't there. They didn't look like prac- tised riders. They were drawing closer. Who were they? The horse in front carried no pack behind its rider. The others, by contrast, had a great deal. They came to a halt. What was happening? The leading rider was pointing towards Reykholt. Were they talking to someone? Snorre sought cover behind a large boulder. Only one of them was talking, the man at the rear. They were by some brush- wood in the marsh. On the edge of it was a tall bush. Were they speaking to someone he couldn't see? Sleipnir wanted to go on. Snorre held the reins tight. They couldn't see him. They turned their horses and rode off in the opposite direction! Five armed men emerged from behind the bush. He started. His heart pounded. The three horsemen rode back the way they'd come with the five men following them. The concealed men had made them return along the same road! Was Reykholt surrounded? He had to return unobserved. What had they done with Margrete? Hope- fully she'd chosen a different road. It was important to get behind the gates as quickly as possible. Every able-bodied man at Reykholt must be summoned. Immediately! Was Orækja one of the five? He strained his eyes. It was impos- sible to recognize any of them. Orækja's black horse wasn't there. But he might have changed horses.

Snorre leant forward, ever watchful of the men a few hundred yards off. He lifted his right leg behind him and tried to slip down the left side of Sleipnir's back and belly. As soon as his feet touched the grass, he took the reins and led the horse towards the gate. He could still see them. They'd stopped, hadn't they? His temples thudded. Did they have people inside Reykholt working for them?

What Snorre couldn't discern was that the leader of the five men was Gissur Thorvaldsson. If Snorre had known this, he might possibly have realized at last what lay in store.

Sixteen years earlier, Gissur had married Snorre's daughter, Ingibjørg. Gissur had been fifteen at the time and Little Jon's best friend. The young Haukdøl had grown up not far from Thingvellir and was a favourite at Reykholt. Even after enmity had reared its head amongst the Sturlungs, he'd sacrificed a great deal for his father-in-law. When, three years previously, Sturla Sighvatsson had driven Snorre out of Reykholt, Gissur let him stay at his own home, Reykir. Gissur tried to effect a reconcilliation between Sturla and Snorre, without success. After Snorre fled to Norway, Gissur was banished by Sturla. This piece of treachery changed Gissur. Until that time he'd been known as a friendly and conciliatory man. Now he'd become cold and calculating. He regarded the Sturlungs as a plague over Iceland. With a well-equipped army, he took Sturla prisoner and personally executed him with an axe.

Back at the gate, Snorre had a final glimpse of the three strangers. They were being followed by the armed riders. He wanted to believe that they were prisoners of the armed men, and had nothing to do with him. He closed the gate and shut his eyes. He tried to conjure up Margrete's face. What if he never saw her again! He got off Sleipnir, dropped the reins and gave the horse a smack on the back. He trotted in a slightly curving route towards the stable.

Should he go indoors? Why spend his time brooding? There was no time to lose, he had to start writing. Could he simply expunge Oraekja from *Snorre's Saga*? Would that make it easier to write? He took a deep breath. Almost everything Orækja had been involved in over the past few years was associated with him. People believed that Orækja usually acted for his father. But it would be right to emphasize how gullible Orækja was. Posterity must know just what he'd had to struggle with as a father.

Snorre went indoors and seated himself at his desk. One of the best examples of Orækja's naivety was the time that Kolbeinn tricked him. Orækja had killed Illugi, stepson of his own half-sister, Thordis. Unfortunately Kolbeinn, Snorre's son-in-law, had been a close friend of Illugi's. Kolbeinn at once demanded a meeting with Orækja on a plain near Stadarholtgård. Immediately, Orækja sent a messenger to Kolbeinn to say that he accepted the challenge. Time and place were agreed upon. Orækja set out. Light of heart and certain of victory, he mounted his horse and told the rest of his men to do the same. Perhaps Kolbeinn would give in? As soon as they faced each other, Kolbeinn would realize that Orækja had much more battle experience. Orækja was almost a head taller than him. Kolbeinn had hardly killed anybody at all. Wouldn't it surprise Kolbeinn that he'd got Sturla with him? The journey took two days on horseback, with one night's sleep under the stars. They were to meet when the sun was at its height. They arrived exactly on time, but Kolbeinn and his henchmen were nowhere to be seen. They waited for the rest of the day. Had there been a misunderstanding? Had Orækja come at the wrong time? He felt an instant's uncertainty, and asked one of the men closest to him. But there wasn't any doubt. They'd come at the correct time. It was Kolbeinn who'd named the hour. Orækja was convinced Kolbeinn would come. Several of Orækja's men left him after a couple of hours. Orækja stood there for a long time and then paced in a wide circle, looking at the sea. The breakers beat against the cliffs, like days, months. In the

dusk he heard the familiar sound of galloping hooves.
Orækja crouched down, listening for how many horses
there might be. The outstretched fingers of his right hand
barely touched the grass. He tilted his head. There were
perhaps eight or ten. No more.

Orækja went across to a couple of men who were
standing by themselves. They'd already made preparations
to leave. They were certain Kolbeinn wouldn't come.
Orækja asked them if now they'd admit that they'd been
wrong. They refused to answer. One lowered his eyes, the
other shrugged his shoulders. Orækja drew his sword. One
of the men, who was looking out for the horses, shouted
that he could see them. There were ten of them. They were
approaching. It was only when the horses were very close
that it was possible to tell if Kolbeinn was one of the riders.
He wasn't. The leader jumped from his horse, ran to Orækja
and handed him a letter. Orækja snatched it and read it
quickly. He said nothing. Several of Orækja's men shouted
that they wanted to know what was in the letter. He handed
it to the man who stood nearest to him. Raising his voice,
the man read out that Kolbeinn was unable to come at
this time, but that he would on a subsequent occasion.
And when that meeting took place, the messenger put in,
Kolbeinn hoped they would be able to agree on what
should be done with the Vestfirdings, who were complain-
ing about Orækja's despotic rule. Orækja asked the messenger, who stood in front of his steaming horse, why
Kolbeinn hadn't come. The messenger replied that he knew
nothing more than was in the letter. Orækja read through
it again, without ending up any the wiser.

Some of Orækja's men on the edges of the group were
openly chortling. Orækja looked around, mounted a flat
rock and told them he regarded Kolbeinn's letter as an

admission that he'd given way and that they would certainly manage to agree about most things. All in all, Kolbeinn was a sensible man. He was his wife's brother, wasn't he? Orækja told the messenger to inform Kolbeinn that he appreciated the letter.

It had been a week since Snorre had met Orækja with Tumi and Sturla at Saudafjell. Snorre had examined the letter for a long time. He had raised it to his nose and sniffed the calfskin and the ink made from gall. The finest of all inks—the shit of the gall wasp on oak leaves, with some iron sulphate added. An ink that would last a thousand years. Snorre had thought it useless to go into these details with his sons. He smelt the ink and established that the letter had indeed been written two days previously. No more, no less. His nostrils quivered eagerly over the letter. The smell of the calfskin disturbed the overall effect a tiny bit, but not enough to cause his fine nose any doubt. Orækja was right. The letter was genuine. Snorre recognized Kolbeinn's handwriting. He paced up and down in front of his son. Finally, Orækja asked what his father was thinking about. He said nothing. He continued his slow perambulation, hands behind his back. All at once he raised his head and looked hard at Orækja. He asked his son why he hadn't done more to establish the reason for Kolbeinn's absence. Orækja's glance started to waver. Snorre shook his head and stamped his foot. For an instant it looked as if he were about to lose his balance. He seated himself on a boulder, gasped for air and clutched at his heart. Orækja bounded across to him, clasped his father and asked if anything was the matter. Snorre pushed his son away and said that he felt perfectly well. Orækja straightened up and asked why his father couldn't believe him. Snorre explained that it wasn't Orækja he couldn't trust, but Kolbeinn. But why had his father doubted that the letter was genuine at first? He'd told his father that it *was* genuine. It was a fact. Snorre reached for his quill. That had been seven days ago.

While Oraekja and Snorre were at Saudafjell, Kolbeinn had a meeting with Gissur at which they planned the details of Snorre's murder. Snorre would never know about this strange meeting that took place on the edges of his own horizon. And the three men from Rome would never get closer to Reykholt. The servants whispered to one another and tried to be glad they were alive. When the priest saw the resolution in the eyes of the men escorting them away from Reykholt, he felt unsure of the strength of his faith. Samuel Ugolino was tall and thin and unintentionally bearded. When they'd set out on the sea crossing from Shetland to Iceland, his razor had fallen into the water. He imagined the reproachful look of his uncle, Pope Gregory IX, if he failed to deliver the letter. The translation of the leader's words, supplied by his servant, Giuseppe Tornelli, convinced him. The man meant what he said. It wasn't his sentiments, or the translation, but the calmness of his face that showed him to be a man who dealt in life and death. The fact that they were emissaries of the pope had made no significant impression. Once again, the priest asked for permission to deliver the letter to Snorre. His servant reluctantly repeated the request and added, on his own initiative, that the priest feared the pope's reaction if the task wasn't fulfilled. The men regarded the thoughtful interpreter and smiled. The interpreter hoped this was a sign of sympathy. Perhaps the men in front of him understood a bit about the pomp and authority that emanated from Pope Gregory IX?

Gregory IX wasn't merely a pope and a count. He was also a member of one of Italy's most powerful families. They had property all the way down to Sardinia. And, oddly enough, the unity in this influential family was uncommonly strong. Now that they also included the pope amongst their number, their self-assurance was formidable. Did the men realize, Tornelli asked, that the pope was supported by both the Franciscan and Dominican orders, that he had set up the Inquisition, that he had brought out a new edition of *Corpus Juris Canonici*, and that, to cap it all, he was the man who was in the process of unifying Italy? They shrugged. He was the man who would become pope and emperor simultaneously, Tornelli continued. Here the priest chipped in and asked if he hadn't translated rather more than he'd said?

'A bit more,' the pious servant replied.

If the three emissaries didn't complete their mission, the pope wouldn't give Ugolino a countship or a bishopric. And if Gregory IX had the least suspicion that his letter hadn't been delivered because Ugolino had been craven, he knew what awaited him. He had personally witnessed how his brother had been treated after the pope had begun to doubt his orthodoxy. His brother hadn't exactly been helped by the strange disease the pope had contracted. He was practically scratching himself to death. In the pope's own opinion, it was the Devil's work. As he was such a devout believer, his trials had to be extra hard. The itching drove him to the edge of insanity. The doctors had tried everything. Now they were putting random ingredients into their medications. Every kind of liquid and oil, herb and powder was essayed. The doctors were threatened with crucifixion if they didn't find something to ease the torture. Gradually, ants of every description began to show an increasing interest in him. He exuded a stench that was totally irresistible to these industrious creatures. In the papal palace he was continually being carried from one end of the room to the other in a sedan chair. And all the time, as the pains grew more and more unendurable, increasing numbers of his courtiers were branded as traitors and familiars of the ants and the Devil. As the day and evening wore on, and before he finally fell asleep, his scribes could hardly keep a tally of the number of times a single individual might be sentenced to death.

A small ray of hope grew in the papal envoys when Gissur asked if he could see the letter. The servants looked imploringly at the priest, who hesitated and then realized he had nothing to lose. Samuel Ugolino carefully removed the letter from the leather container with the pope's monogram on its seal. He read the letter aloud. It was addressed to Snorre. He read it first in Latin, then had the translation read for them. It was the final paragraph that aroused the greatest interest. Here, Snorre was enjoined to unite Iceland and Norway and bring about a new Crusade for Jerusalem, which was now under the control of the Holy Roman Emperor, Frederick II—an emperor who, in the remainder of the letter, was styled a 'traitor'. He had been 'impudent enough to allow himself to be crowned in the pope's Rome in 1220'. Frederick II had reached a compromise with the infidels concerning the future of Jerusalem. At the very end was a reference to Sigurd I Magnusson's victorious Crusade more than a century before, in which several Icelanders had participated. According to the pope, Rome was receiving ever more pious pilgrims from Norway and Iceland. Snorre's name was regularly mentioned to the pope as the only man with sufficient influence in both countries. After the letter had been read in both Latin and Icelandic, there was silence. The pope's messengers looked expectantly at Gissur Thorvaldsson. Gissur asked to see the letter. The priest asked if he understood Latin.

'A bit,' he answered in Icelandic. After an even longer silence, the priest asked if he might get the letter delivered, preferably personally.

'It's too late,' was the answer. The priest looked as if he'd been struck by a fatal arrow. They were asked how they'd made the long journey to Iceland and Reykholt. Tornelli did the talking. The priest was in no condition to speak. His first sentences were hesitant and disjointed. But when Tornelli noticed that one of the men, Eirik Torfinnson, had a crucifix inside his cloak, his words came more easily. In the company of three other Icelandic pilgrims, Torfinnson had visited Rome to see the graves of the martyrs Peter and Paul before heading back north again. The pope, St Peter's successor and leader of the mother church, His Holiness himself, had blessed the mission. The servant repeated that it was the pope himself, the 'Padre', who wanted the letter delivered. Eirik corrected him politely and said that the Icelandic word was 'Páfi'. The papal emissaries couldn't conceal their surprise at this precise correction. Now it seemed almost as if the servant had a personal need to give a detailed description of their trying journey. Rigours, which until that moment he'd tried to forget, now welled up within him. The telling obviously had a soothing effect in itself. Tornelli asked if any of them had been on a pilgrimage to Rome and seen the palace of the Hospitallers of St John of Jerusalem with its wonderful view of the Imperial Fora, and the Colosseum, the Basilica of Maxentius, Trajan's Column, the Arch of Titus, the Aventine Hill and the palaces of Augustus and Domitian; he managed to mention all these before he was interrupted. They wanted to hear about the journey, and not his homesickness.

He described the journey northwards to the coast of Normandy, near the town which today is called Le Havre, in some detail. From there, they took ship for Shetland and the Faroe Islands, before landing on Iceland's southwest coast. But how had they reached Normandy? It was Gissur who asked. He had a brother on a pilgrimage to Rome and he was interested in how long it would take him to get home. They had travelled from Rome to Terni, then to Perugia and on to beautiful Florence before arriving at Lucca, where they saw the Volto Santo crucifix with its healing powers. The servant took a small lead model of it from a kerchief and handed it to Gissur, who cast a quick glance at it before giving it back. After Lucca, they'd made for the Ligurian coast and Genoa. In order to avoid the Alps, they'd followed the coastal road to Marseille and then the river Rhône to Lyon. For several weeks, they rode along the Saône to Dijon, where they stayed at a monastery to nurse the priest who'd caught pneumonia. After he'd recovered, they travelled to Paris where they lived at the university. Here, they had personally seen a book that had been presented by the wise and pious Icelander, Jon Loptsson. From Paris they'd ridden to Bayeux.

'A couple of days later, we sailed for the Shetland Islands,' put in Samuel Ugolino. He must be able to persuade them. They were, when all was said and done, fellow believers even if they weren't at all like him. He had to inform them of the great misfortune that had befallen Jerusalem. Christendom itself was being eradicated. Was there any better argument than that! They'd heard of Frederick II, hadn't they? Frederick had grown up in Sicily, learning Arabic and studying the art and culture of the Orient. His marriage to the daughter of the Frank who had conquered Jerusalem had made Frederick II king of the city. He cooperated with Egypt's ruler, Sultan al-Kamil, over Jerusalem's future. Just like Frederick II, Sultan Saladin—a Kurd and a

Muslim—believed that the Holy City should be open to all religions, and he kept to his word! Saladin had been presumptuous enough to send the Crusader King Richard the Lionheart peaches, pears and crates of snow from Mount Hermon to ease his fever. This couldn't have been from kindness but out of a desire to humiliate.

On 18 February 1229, the Holy Roman Emperor and the Sultan of Cairo came to a compromise about Jerusalem which opened the city to people of various faiths.

The pope and Ugolino compared Frederick II to the Byzantines—traitors who permitted different religions to exist side by side in Constantinople until the Fourth Crusade put a stop to it. With his own eyes, Ugolino had proudly beheld the spoils from Byzantium outside St Mark's Basilica in Venice. The bronze horses above the west door of the basilica snorted and trampled in triumph. A little below it, the sculpture of Heracles racing away with the Erymanthian Boar. All this had been plundered from the Hagia Sophia cathedral in Constantinople, after the Crusaders had drunk from the holy chalices, smashed the icons and loaded gold and silverware, candlesticks and gilded sculptures on to mules which staggered beneath their weight.

'Frederick II has entered into a compact with the Devil,' Ugolino shouted. 'Jerusalem's dignity and honour are at stake. Is Jerusalem to burn in hell? Without us Christian brothers raising a finger? You, my Icelandic brothers, are a part of this army. Where do we want to end up after our own miserable lives are over? In heaven or in hell?'

He was so close to Snorre Sturlason's home! It couldn't be more than a couple of stone's throws away. Should he try to run from the Icelanders and hurl the container and its letter across the ramparts? He glanced at them. They'd be able to kill him before he'd got half way. Ugolino dismissed the thought. God would have to help him. Why wouldn't they let him meet Snorre? Was he the one who'd sent these five men out?

He spoke with a fervour and avidity which made it hard for the interpreter to keep up. But where had Ugolino seen Frederick II? Gissur demanded impatiently. Ugolino said he'd witnessed this would-be emperor ride off with his court across the Alps in the direction of the Rhine. That was when he'd seen the sort of people this libertine surrounded himself with. In addition to a vast caravan of horses and mules which hauled a fully-equipped kitchen and a small library, part of the national treasury, as well as weapons, ammunition and the trappings of an entire chancellery, he'd had a sizeable zoo in the rear. The animals which couldn't be put in cages walked in single file. Elephants, giraffes, camels and even a leopard trudged along, and above the large animals monkeys jumped from back to back, and after the crowd of animals came several oriental dancing women, gyrating to the tambours of an orchestra of jugglers!

'And this "emperor" is supposed to be learned!' Ugolino cried.

The knowledge that Reykholt lay behind the nearest hillock impelled the priest to exhort everyone to a concluding prayer. They stood obediently by the side of their horses. The priest prayed in Latin, his eyes closed.

Gissur wouldn't hear any more. He said tersely that the papal envoys had to get going. Two of his men would take them to a ship that was bound for Lindisfarne in northeast England. Farewell. Ugolino tore the letter out of the interpreter's hands, threw himself on his knees before the Icelandic leader and beseeched him to deliver the letter to

Snorre. All dignity had gone. The interpreter looked away. The other servant, who was holding the leather cylinder, gazed at the ground. The priest began to weep. Words and emotions ran mingling down his cheeks without making Gissur any more pliant.

The gabbling priest was caught up under both arms by the Icelanders and placed on his horse.

'Don't worry about it, not everyone's lucky enough to arrive at the right moment,' Gissur said, and tore up the letter with the pope's signature on it.

'Hurry along, and get aboard in time,' was the last thing the priest heard, admittedly not in a language he understood. He swooned, falling on to his horse's neck, but managed to hold on. The horse began to move. His two servants quickly mounted their horses and rode to Borg, where the ship was waiting.

A week later, the papal delegation had left Iceland. They rode for three weeks from Lindisfarne to London. On his horse, Ugolino saw the pope's merciless eyes before him the whole way. He could even imagine his voice, gruff and husky. He imagined the pope with dread as he rode into Canterbury, south-east of London. The archbishop of Canterbury received them kindly. After they'd been shown round the beautiful cathedral, the archbishop told them he had a piece of sad news to impart. Ugolino thought it concerned the place they'd just seen, where holy Thomas à Becket had been murdered in 1170. The archbishop faced Ugolino, grasped both his hands in his own and looked at him. He couldn't avoid noticing Ugolino's crooked nose. In a grave voice, the archbishop announced that Pope Gregory IX was dead. Ugolino asked the archbishop to repeat the words he'd just spoken. Had he heard them right?

'Your uncle, Pope Gregory the Ninth, is dead.'

Ugolino closed his eyes. For a few moments, he wanted to be alone with his thoughts. Ugolino wasn't by any means bereft of ability, but that didn't mean he didn't depend on a large amount of luck for most of his success. After a while, he opened his eyes again. The archbishop said that he was impressed by the strength the priest had shown after receiving the sorrowful tidings. Ugolino asked the archbishop if it were possible to buy a bottle of Thomas à Becket's diluted blood. It was supposed to be the best cure for everything. The road back to Rome was still a long one.

The ship they took foundered on the rocks off the English coast. The papal envoys drowned before help arrived. Here ends the story of the three messengers Snorre never met.

Snorre stared at the gate he'd shut. How could he imagine he'd simply be able to sit down and write? What had happened? Had the men outside the ramparts ridden off towards Surtshellir? He was ashen-faced. What did the men out there want with him? He opened the gate a little. He hoped they hadn't done anything to her. He opened the gate wide. They weren't there.

He closed his eyes, opened them. Yes, he really was awake. His face regained its normal colour. An auk-like bird waddled past just in front of him. He recognized it immediately. It was a fine specimen. It was rare to see them in the vicinity of Reykholt, they usually stayed near the sea. The bill was sturdy. The bird was white underneath and black on top. Its head was black with a large white patch beside each eye. The wings were short—they looked like flippers. It couldn't fly. As a boy, he'd taken hundreds of great auk eggs at Oddi. The stubby wings moved constantly. The bird lurched, zig-zagging in front of him. It reached to his knees. Snorre smiled at its helpless flapping. He closed the gate. Before getting hold of Kyrre, he wanted to speak to the priest. He walked calmly to the small church.

Margrete would certainly have got back home. Surely, there was nothing to prevent them seeing each other again soon? If he saw Kyrre on the way, he wouldn't say anything at all. The stable boy mustn't discern the slightest trace of anxiety in him. He would merely nod and move on. Why hadn't he let the great auk come in? He returned to the gate, pulled the bolt back carefully, opened the gate and looked out.

Meat, Snorre thought. The next time Margrete came to Reykholt, they'd have some great auk.

'Come in,' Snorre called.

He opened the gate wide. There was a squawk. The bird was being crushed behind the gate. The great auk extricated itself and pecked at his right thigh. He looked about him. Was it a trap? It was alone. With one cut of his sword, he could have parted the bird's head from its body. All that would have been left was some blood and two pieces of meat and bone. Quite unafraid, and with ever increasing force, the bird hacked at his thigh. He tried to push it away by aiming its head towards the gateway. Why couldn't it hurry up and go in? He'd find some food for it. The auk made a stab at Snorre's left thigh. He dodged to the side. The bird missed. Once, when he'd been on a long trip, he'd strangled a great auk to get some fresh meat. It had tasted good! The bird pecked at him again. This time it found its mark. He turned his back on it. The pecking stopped. He faced it warily. With its eyes fixed on Snorre, it lunged straight at him and caught him between the thighs. Snorre screamed. He raised his right arm. A cloud forced its way in front of the sun. The bird's silhouette became even clearer. He wrapped his arms around it. The struggling bird jabbed at Snorre's cheek. The auk was heavier than he'd imagined. He staggered through the open gate. With his right leg, he managed to pull the gate closed behind him. If there was anyone out there who thought he was foolish enough to chase a great auk outside the gate, they were wrong.

Three people stood hidden behind the church. They smiled at one another. Snorre managed to carry the bird over to the church. It was all he could do to hold the writhing head with both his hands. His cheek was bleeding.

The bird pecked him several times. He shouted and struck at it. The blow missed. He fell sideways. The auk waddled across the yard. The dog came running up. The bird moved straight towards it. In one leap the dog got the auk by the throat. The jaws closed around its neck. It tried to beat its two little parodies of wings. It had never flown. A short time later it lay still in the yard. It died without knowing fear, just as the last great auk would six hundred years later. Its blood dried fast on the dog's grey muzzle. Snorre swore and bawled at the dog, which stood whining at its feeding bowl.

Snorre couldn't get up. He looked over at the church. He heard someone whistle. He saw no sign of Kyrre. He stared at the church again. The three people behind it pressed close together. Nobody smiled now. What if the old man had seen them?

They saw that he was trying to get onto his hands and knees. He hadn't bumped his head but he felt giddy. He didn't want people to see him lying like this. As soon as he'd raised himself on to all fours, he fell over on his side again. He stretched his right leg, then his left. He straightened his arms. His hips were stiff. He shook his head, coughed, gazed around. Should he call for help? He'd rather die!

He breathed heavily, he hadn't broken anything. Why not be thankful for that? He sat on his haunches. That went all right. There was a hammering at his temples. What was wrong with him? He felt the sweat on his face and in his armpits. He felt dizzy. At length, he managed to raise his great body. Snorre swayed but managed to prop himself up against the church wall. He ought to be spared the need to drag a body about. His head was more than enough.

Snorre shook his head. He no longer felt shaky. He looked across at the lifeless great auk. The dog had spoilt the meat. He must speak to the priest—talkative he might be, but he knew a lot about animals. He could ask the priest if he didn't think a great auk so far from the coast was strange. In the course of the conversation he would ask the priest if he'd noticed anything else unusual. If an opening presented itself, he would drop a hint about Torkild. Not with a serious expression, he'd rather appear light-hearted. His arms behind his back, Snorre slowly climbed the steps of the lovely church. On the top step he drew breath. He turned his face to the side. He lifted his gaze in the direction of the towering bulks of Eiriksjøkull and Langjøkull, with their enormous glaciers. Hopefully, she'd managed to reach safety by riding that way. A mouse ran past the bottom of the steps. It disappeared into the yellowing grass. The door wasn't locked. He opened it, entered and closed the door behind him. There was no one visible in the aisle or in the pews. The priest must be in the room behind the vestry. The silver candlesticks and the runner Hallveig had woven were still as she'd left them. Snorre hadn't been inside the church since Hallveig's funeral. A silver vase contained two rowan twigs, thick with berries. It looked as if they'd been there a few days.

Had someone in that strange group brought the auk along as a living larder? It was a possible explanation. Snorre stood a moment in front of the vestry. He glanced up at the pale woodcarving of Jesus, hanging on the cross, with his crown of thorns and his head tilted to the left. Was it the priest or was it Torkild who'd fashioned that animated figure with axe and knife and chisel? He studied the wooden sculpture for a long time. How had it been possible to depict such pain with those lifeless tools? He walked hesitantly towards the back room. Only after he'd opened the door did he shout for Arnbjørn, the priest. There was no reply. Nothing is so silent as an empty church. He went down the aisle and tore open the door. He took the steps in one bound and landed on his right foot. The ankle took his whole weight. After three tottering paces, he fell forward. His arms stretched out sideways. His stomach hit the ground first, then his forehead. He heard laughter. He turned.

So there they were! It was Gyda who was laughing. Kyrre lowered his hand over her mouth. There was also the young boy who helped Kyrre in the stable. He didn't know him. The boy might be about fifteen. Each time Snorre came face to face with him, he blushed.

Snorre recalled only too well the last time he'd seen Kyrre and the blonde boy together. Snorre had been riding back from Borg. Outside the ramparts at Reykholt, he'd spotted four horses and two young men. He'd slowed from a gallop to a gentle trot before stopping and concealing himself behind some bushes. To begin with, he couldn't believe his eyes. Two of the horses had horns tied to their heads. With these they were butting each other until the blood ran. His horses! Two of his best breeding stallions.

He'd pushed the branches aside and galloped up at full speed. Kyrre and the youth weren't able to escape that time. As soon as he reached the stallions engaged in their mortal combat, he recognized the other two horses—a couple of tethered mares. The sight and smell of the mares had made the stallions want to kill each other. As soon as he surprised them, the youth fell to his knees and bowed his head. He expected a beating. Kyrre stood erect and took all the blame on himself. Snorre told him to hold his tongue and separate the two foaming horses. The boy got up and ran over to the mares, led them away and tied them securely to a post a good way off. If Sleipnir had been one of the two bleeding stallions, he would have done more than just weep.

Now, Kyrre and the youth came to Snorre's aid. Snorre managed to rise by holding on to Kyrre's arm. As soon as Snorre was on his feet, Kyrre moved aside. Why this consideration on Kyrre's part? Some feel compassion for those awaiting the executioner. Kyrre had heard the rumours. Gyda had told him everything.

'What were you all laughing at?' he shouted. They stared at the ground. He was on the point of asking Kyrre why people were hiding. What were they frightened of? How many were left on the estate? He glanced at the other two fools. Was he going to ask his stable boy what was happening on his own farm? Of course not. The youth looked down at his hand that was clutching the auk by the neck. Snorre told Kyrre to stay behind. He'd talk to the others later. Kyrre seemed self-confident. He'd assumed a strength Snorre hadn't seen in him before. Kyrre said that, unfortunately, he had to go. Snorre told him to stay where he was. The other two stood there to see what happened to Kyrre. Kyrre would have to answer.

'Tell me why you were laughing!' he yelled.

Snorre tried to catch hold of Kyrre's smock, but he pulled loose and jumped to the side. Gyda didn't move out of the way quickly enough. Snorre managed to grasp her with both arms. He was crimson with fury and put his arm around her neck and squeezed. Gyda went white in the face. Her legs gave way, she lost her breath. No cry or scream escaped her lips. She fell backwards with Snorre on top of her, and landed head first. Everyone heard the sound of her head hitting the ground. Snorre lay heavily on top of her. He managed to roll over to the side. He got to his knees. She wasn't breathing. He slapped her. She lay motionless. He slapped her again. The eyelids didn't open. He began to shout at her. Kyrre's face was white. The young boy stood next to Kyrre. His mouth was open. Had Snorre killed his servant girl? He looked at her closed eyes. He shook her. He turned to the two others.

'Well, do something!'

Kyrre raised his arms sideways. The boy stood behind him. Snorre bent over her face. He tilted his head. Perhaps she was breathing after all? Never in his life had he killed another person. And had he now murdered a cripple, a harmless girl, in his own farmyard? He crouched on his hands and knees and stared at her. The other two came a couple of steps closer. He shut his eyes. He heard his own heavy breathing. He yelled. He opened his eyes a crack. Wasn't there a tear under one eyelid? And another. There were several under the other lid. He shook her. He bent over her and pushed open her eyes with his big fingers.

'Make her live!'

Gyda hadn't dared open her eyes for fear of looking straight into his face, feeling his breath and seeing his furious expression. Finally, the old man rose with great difficulty.

At that, she opened her eyes. Kyre ran the couple of steps to her, knelt and brushed the hair away from her face. Snorre looked at her, nodded, dried his tears, cursed and went to the main house without turning, opened the door and stepped over the high threshold. He glanced out a couple of times. He could see them raising her to her feet between them. She limped more than usual and was crying. He paced the floor before looking out again. Perhaps he should ask Kyrre where the priest was? It would seem reasonable for him to ask. They'd seen him entering the church, after all. And it would give the impression that the lord of the manor still had control of himself and the life of his estate. Snorre felt it was wise to keep in contact with the priest. Hopefully, it would make it harder for Arnbjørn to tell tales about the secret tunnels Snorre had told him about.

Not many weeks before, he'd surprised Arnbjørn in an embarassing situation. Snorre had been absent for a few days inspecting Bessastadir. He'd got a rough idea of how things stood with his stock of cows. The weather was fine and the trip home went quicker than planned. At close to midnight he got back to his house, unobserved. Next morning, in good spirits, he took the subterranean tunnel to the pool. A new day had dawned and he was 'putting his best foot forward', he told himself. He was anticipating the pleasure of lowering himself into the water.

Just as he was about to open the door to the pool, he stopped. He had the feeling somebody was there. He opened the door warily. A man was trying to scramble out of the pool. Obviously, the man had heard him. His skin was white, almost grey to Snorre's eyes. At first, he didn't know who it was. He'd never seen a more naked person. The priest stood there in all his imperfection, reconciled to his fate, caught in a mercilessly disdainful gaze. The landscape about them shone in his brown eyes. His hands were thin and wan and not quite so grey as the rest of his body. There was not much to say, either for Snorre or Arnbjørn, who was staring at the ground. His face was adorned with a straggly, blonde moustache. Life, it seemed, had washed away all trace of expression. As a rule, the face seemed built for hiding itself away, a blank wall with a pale network of veins, where trivial ideas could revolve freely, before the need to collect his thoughts for the next prayer.

Arnbjørn had probably reckoned he'd get away with it. His eyes were like craters. The lined face contained something that could only be a smirk. The odd hair or bristle emerged from warts, birthmarks, nose and ears. His ears were two lobes close to his head. The details were easier to make out when the blush sank down his body and disappeared into the grass and the earth, and the paleness returned. Snorre's look pinned the priest to the spot. Arnbjørn stood there, without showing any sign of retrieving his clothes and dressing himself. He was waiting for Snorre to say something. The priest was getting cold. Above the pool, the vault of the sky showed its geography of clouds and mobile continents. Snorre saw a greylag goose flapping towards the pool. Arnbjørn managed to glimpse a fleeting shadow before he saw it disappear in the direction of the horses' enclosure.

Snorre's eyes settled back on the priest. Gooey, yellowish-grey birdshit ran from his hair, over his eyebrows and moustache, and onto the priest's left shoulder. He lifted his right hand to wipe it away.

'I suppose you noticed where that came from?' Snorre asked.

Without waiting for an answer, he turned on his heel and and passed through the door, shaking his head. His bath would have to wait. The priest stood there. A few steps along the tunnel, a smile crept over Snorre's face. Athough he decidedly disliked the priest, he would never have believed that two days later Arnbjørn was to betray him in the most brutal way possible, without so much as a single prayer passing his lips.

Snorre ran his hand across his face, cleared his throat and sat down at his desk. Should he waste even one word on the priest? No sooner had the base of his spine settled into the back of his chair, than he got up again. He wanted to put on his brown jacket with its belt and fur trimming. The cuffs and collar were of fox pelt.

It was a pity no one could see him. He looked truly elegant, not overdressed as he'd been for Margrete's visit. Now he would write about Orækja. He'd thought enough. Had he been too unkind to Arnbjørn down at the pool? The next time he saw the priest, he ought to suggest a game of 'King's Table', *hnefatafl*. The priest loved *hnefatafl*. Arnbjørn had given him the board. Each time they'd played, he'd offered to let Snorre play with the big army to make him tractable. In Snorre's opinion games were the dullest things imaginable. The world was more than enough to occupy him. That first year Snorre was convinced the priest hadn't a single base thought.

The day following the embarrassing episode by the pool, Arnbjørn asked him if he'd ever heard of Ottar, and then if Snorre believed there'd been any notable saga writers prior to himself. Snorre looked quizzically at him, as he didn't know what these questions were leading up to. Surely Snorre had heard of Ottar? Arnbjørn reiterated, 'the man who lived further north than any other Norwegian', and had ventured into the White Sea before sailing along the Norwegian coast to Skiringssal in Vestfold four centuries previously. Snorre didn't answer. Surely Snorre knew that Ottar had travelled to Hedeby, in what we now call Schleswig-Holstein, before he sailed to England and took service with King Alfred the Great? Was it Snorre's opinion that Ottar wasn't a great historian? Did he believe this in order to appear in a better light himself? Before Snorre had a chance to answer, Arnbjørn asked why Snorre hadn't mentioned Ottar's travels and descriptions in his works. Did he know that King Alfred had welcomed Ottar and his works and permitted them to appear in his own translation of the late Roman writer and historian Orosius? Surely Snorre knew that the English king had considered it perverse for a world history not to contain anything from the regions north of the Alps?

Snorre asked if it mightn't be time for the man of God to prepare for compline. Surely he hadn't forgotten those who were waiting for the last office of the day? And before Arnbjørn could reply, Snorre reminded the priest that in addition to compline, matins and vespers should be heard every day in church. Originally, Benedict of Nursia had believed that six offices should be observed each day. Perhaps that was a little excessive, but surely the Reykholt priest should be able to manage three?

The priest showed no sign of rising.

His words came slowly, as if they had to be chewed an extra time before leaving his mouth. Arnbjørn lived alone, and when he'd finally found someone to talk to, he was loath to relinquish him.

Snorre was feeling tired. He was jolted awake when Arnbjørn asked if he had actually visited Re, where the final scene of his *Heimskringla* was played out. Snorre explained that he hadn't been to Stiklestad either, although he'd come close to it. He'd had no desire to see the place where St Olav had drawn his last breath. He glanced at the horrified priest. Snorre said he thought it was getting late. Arnbjørn didn't take the hint.

'I want to be alone,' Snorre said.

Arnbjørn walked rapidly to the door, opened it and walked towards the church without turning.

Snorre began to wonder what his last words on earth would be. The ones he'd put in the mouths of various characters in *Heimskringla* would raise expectations of his own valediction. Just before Erling Skjalgsson was cut down, he said: 'Face to face the eagles fight.' That, in any case, was what Snorre had written. Or the young Jomsviking, Sigurd, son of Bue Digre: 'Not all the Jomsvikings are dead yet.' Tormod Kolbrunarskald tore out the arrow, bits of flesh still clinging to it, with the words: 'Right well the king has fed us, the cockles of my heart are still fat.' Could anything have been better said?

Snorre took out his writing materials. He grasped his quill and let his gaze wander over some of his own works. It annoyed him that he didn't have the lays to King Sverre's nephews, King Inge Bårdsson and Jarl Håkon Galen, before him. The jarl had been extremely pleased. Snorre was presented with a sword, a shield and a coat of mail, as well as an invitation to Norway. But the jarl died, and the journey was postponed. That was how he'd begun. Writing poems for princes had been the start. Then he'd been nominated lawspeaker and leader of the legislative assembly of the Althing for a couple of years. The writing came to a halt. Then, after his first term as lawspeaker, he travelled to Norway. In his waterproof leather bag, he carried his *Háttatal*, one hundred and two variations of the old poetic metres, as a gift for King Håkon. Håkon Håkonsson had just become king. The boy ruled together with Duke Skúli.

Snorre was well received. The first winter he read his poems to the chieftains at Tønsberg. What an atmosphere! The following summer he rode to Håkon Galen's widow, Kristin. He read to her with power and feeling, and was presented with fine gifts. That was more than twenty years ago.

From there he went to Konghelle to see the place where Jon Loptsson had grown up. Jon and his father had witnessed the assault on the Wends at Konghelle in 1135. Sigurd the Crusader had also lived there. Snorre wanted to see as much as possible. Some months earlier, he'd accepted an invitation from Duke Skúli. After the duke had heard him recite, he'd offered him the opportunity to write the saga of the Norwegian kings. From Konghelle he took ship for Nidaros. On the way he saw Hafrsfjord and the flat landscape with the Ryfylke moors in the background. At Nidaros, he almost finished his history. The following summer, he continued writing at Bjørgvin, and he completed it in Iceland. At Bjørgvin, he'd recieved various expensive presents, including the silver-inlaid chair on which he now sat. And it was at Bjørgvin that he made his most fateful promise to the king: Håkon gave him the rank of royal vassal, the highest amongst Norwegian chieftains, in return for bringing Iceland under the rule of the Norwegian king and Norwegian law.

He must make sure to write about his meetings with King Håkon. He remembered them still. It was fortunate for him that he possessed a reasonably good memory even now.

The first time Snorre went to Norway, King Håkon was fifteen. That was in 1220. Each time the young monarch said anything, he would glance at Skúli to make sure he hadn't said anything amiss. Snorre noticed his curly, blonde hair and his downy upper lip. But the king made

no more impact than that. He was by no means unconge-
nial, but he was invisible in a way because he seemed to be
nothing more than Skúli's shadow. At the beginning of the
audience with the young king, Snorre made an effort to
be patient and polite. The boy was a king after all. Snorre
kept explaining to him what had already been discussed
and agreed with Skúli. Gradually, both he and Skúli ignored
Håkon. The king was a person they didn't rate. The boy
spoke less and less whenever they met, until he said nothing. The power lay with Skúli. That was where Snorre's
interests lay.

King Inge Bårdsson had accepted Håkon as the king's
son ever since his birth and had brought him up at the
court. Even after Håkon had been accepted as king by the
Ørething, Inge's half-brother, Skúli, had never seriously
accepted him as monarch. Officially, he did so—anything
else would have been unthinkable. Skúli was nominated
as Håkon's guardian, his regent, and he also got a third of
the realm with its revenues.

Snorre and Skúli enjoyed talking about the writing of
history, the Roman historian Suetonius, the rules for good
lays and the Clerical Party's king, Filippus, as if the fifteen-
year-old understood nothing at all. The young king walked
behind the two of them, listening. On one occasion the
king had asked Snorre if the skald realized that his son,
Jon, had been born in the same year as him, in 1204, the
year the Crusaders took Constantinople.

Even after the power-seeking Sigurd Ribbung had surrendered to King Håkon in 1227, it was still always Skúli
that Snorre approached. The fact that Håkon had married
Skúli's daughter and the relationship between king and
duke was amicable for a time made little difference. Håkon
realized early on that Skúli wanted the crown. In 1237,

Skúli received a dukedom from King Håkon. The appointment did nothing to moderate Skúli's plans. Two years later, open warfare broke out between the two of them. Skúli took the title of king at the Ørething. The decisive battle took place near Helgeseter Priory in 1241. The duke was left lying on the field of battle. The man, who together with the king had ruled Norway with such skill, was dead. But Håkon fared no worse on his own.

Snorre wouldn't live to see all the king's successes. Håkon not only made laws banning blood feuds, he built churches and fortresses in Oslo, Håkonshallen in Bergen and the Trondenes Church, founded Marstrand and Ragnhildarholm near Konghelle, concluded the first mercantile accord with the Hanseatic town of Lübeck and made a treaty with Novgorod to safeguard peace in the north. His influence was felt far and wide. An English chronicler describes how Louis IX of France offered him command of the French Crusader fleet, and that the pope wanted him as Holy Roman Emperor. The then incumbent, the heretic Frederick II, had to be deposed by all possible means.

It was only after Snorre's second visit to King Håkon that he realized how the first one had been viewed by the king. Twenty years had elapsed between their first and second meetings. Now it was Håkon who did the talking.

When he arrived at Bjørgvin in 1239, he began to understand that everything had changed in the power balance between Håkon and Skúli. Skúli's new dukedom clearly meant nothing. Snorre had just come from Nidaros, where he'd been staying with Skúli's son, Peter.

'A fine ship you have there, is that the one Skúli gave you?' It was the first thing the king asked. 'I want to speak to you alone. We'll go hunting together.'

'Isn't Duke Skúli coming too?' Snorre blurted out, before he'd had time to hide his uncertainty.

'He's got duties to attend to,' the king replied, as Skúli looked away.

Snorre wanted to preface his second visit to the now-adult king with a description of the royal visage. There was no longer any fluff on his upper lip, but a thin, well-trimmed moustache beneath a pair of large, clever eyes. He was beardless. The curly, blonde hair of the thirty-five year-old was exactly as it had been when he was fifteen. Their meeting took place a year before open warfare broke out between the king and Skúli.

'That would be an honour, but I've never liked hunting.'

The king regarded him balefully.

'Unfortunately, I'm also plagued with awful pains in my back and legs, they swell up.'

'In that case, we'll meet at Munkeliv Abbey,' Håkon said, 'and afterwards we'll inspect a merchantman from Lübeck, it's just tied up at the wharf. I dare say, Master Skald, sea air won't do you any harm'

While Snorre was wondering what the king was going to tell him next day, Håkon added that they would have a banquet afterwards. The positive manner in which the invitation was given, made Snorre proffer his thanks. The king turned and walked easily towards his main residence. Snorre looked in Skúli's direction. Surely his old friend had time to stop and talk to him? Skúli gazed from the king to Snorre and back again. The king asked Skúli to attend him. They had something important to discuss, he announced loudly. Skúli looked hesitantly at Snorre. Håkon's arm gestured expansively for Skúli and he smiled at him as if they were the heartiest of friends. Snorre had expected Skúli to turn down the king's suggestion. He didn't. Skúli followed his son-in-law like a well-trained dog, without even a nod in Snorre's direction. Neither did the duke pay him a visit before his meeting with the king the following day. Snorre was at the abbey at the appointed time. King Håkon was already there. Alone. Snorre glanced cautiously around for signs of guards.

'Are you looking for someone?' the king asked.

'No.'

'I hear you've visited the lodging where Little Jon was murdered.'

Snorre couldn't say anything.

'I wanted to say that I've heard so many good things about your son.'

This unlooked-for amiability made Snorre's features take on an uncertain cast. The king was being uncommonly formal, pausing between each word.

'He was very important in strengthening the relationship between our two countries,' said the king.

There was a long pause before Snorre said, 'I've heard that you're married to Skúli's daughter, Margrete.'

'That was sixteen years ago,' the king said, smiling, and then added, 'do you like the name?'

Snorre stared at the king's beardless chin. The question was odd in the extreme. Did he know something about Snorre's affair with Margrete? It wasn't inconceivable.

Snorre replied as dispassionately as he could, 'It's a beautiful name, but why did you send my nephew and brother against me the year before last? And why have you asked me to come?'

The king turned to him, came a few steps closer and stood before him, legs apart.

'You heard yourself how hollow that sounded. You have accepted money and a title without delivering your side of the bargain. It's twenty years since we entered our agreement. Iceland will become part of Norway whether you like it or not.'

'Sighvatr and Sturla tried to kill me.'

'I ordered them to bring you back here alive, that's rather different. But as we're on the subject of life and death—I'm in the process of creating a new law at the Ørething, to outlaw blood feuds. Wouldn't that be useful in Iceland as well? Predators only kill when they have to—that's obviously not the case with you people.'

Snorre would willingly have put an entire firmament together just to get away. He stood there. Nothing is more surprising than speechlessness in a man who's always had much to say. Although he couldn't see any of the king's guards or servants in the vicinity, he had no doubt that they were close by. As always, he believed that his skill with words and his experience would rescue him. His self-assurance irritated the king. The man before him would lose his life as soon as he gave the order. To suffer your own self-satisfaction is one thing. But that of others!

'So far, you haven't delivered anything that you promised. You have always underestimated me. That will be a bigger problem for you than for me. I've always known what you and Skúli have been up to. Those days are over now. If you really want my friendship, you can tell me if there's anything in the rumours that Skúli wants to proclaim himself king.'

'How can I answer that? You've stopped me from speaking to him alone.'

'Are you a coward?'

'That's for others to judge, but here I stand without weapons or an army.'

The king wondered if the skald really understood who was in charge of the situation. He took a deep breath and registered that the man before him had aged considerably. His movements were heavy and slow. The last time they'd met, he'd studied every detail of the appearance of this poet and major chieftain, of whom he'd heard so much. He'd had great respect for Snorre, far too great to be upset at being ignored. Now, he'd put on a lot of weight, and looked considerably less well groomed. The king did not attach undue importance to his untrimmed beard, or that he wasn't wearing his finest clothes, but he disliked his complete lack of humility. Didn't he realize that he'd only just managed to escape from Iceland with his life intact? Did he believe he was immortal? Or that he wasn't living on sufferance? The king leant towards Snorre, fixed him with his eyes, smiled and said in a seemingly friendly voice:

'How is your son Orækja?' There was a small pause. 'I hear he's been on a pilgrimage to Rome. Perhaps he'll find that beneficial. I recall sentencing Sturla to a pilgrimage to make him less brutal. He was whipped from one Roman church to the next, but it did him no good. I haven't heard anything of Orækja recently. Is he still alive?'

Snorre shifted in his chair. He looked out across his desk. He mused, and then repeated the exchange one more time. As if the king hadn't known that Orækja was alive. He remembered that he'd been about to ask if the king realized what Sturla had done to Orækja. He said nothing. He didn't want to seem soft-hearted in front of the king. Sturla Sighvatsson's cowardice and cruelty would be set down in writing. If he didn't do that, the whole thing could be forgotten in a few years.

In September 1237, Sturla and Sighvatr had assembled a large army to take Reykholt. Snorre's nephew Sturla was its commander, but Sighvatr lent his son his wholehearted support. They wanted to be the undisputed leaders of Iceland. To betray an uncle and brother was of no concern to them. On the contrary, the fact that they were acting for King Håkon made them even more decisive and determined. The king had had enough of Snorre's evasions.

Orækja assembled an army of six hundred men in four days and rode as fast as he could towards Reykholt. At Saudafjell, Orækja left most of his forces and pushed on to Reykholt with seven men. There, Snorre was consulting his brother, Thordr, and other chieftains. Orækja suggested that they immediately ride north towards Sturla. Nobody paid any attention to him. Not even his father. As a condition for supporting Snorre, Thordr and the other chieftains demanded that Orækja 'should not take part in any capacity'. His father thanked Orækja for turning up and told him to go home. Orækja asked if that really was his father's wish. Snorre nodded. Orækja didn't look at the other men as he walked out. As soon as his son was out of the room, Snorre and Thordr agreed that Snorre would give up Reykholt and let Thordr live there until further notice. Maybe this move would make Sturla and Sighvatr keep away from Reykholt?

Snorre went south, in the opposite direction to his son. He sought refuge at Bessastadir. Sturla rode into Reykholt and took over the estate. Thordr just stood by and let him do it. Orækja shouted that his father had to understand that Sturla and Sighvatr were acting for the Norwegian king. They wanted to kill him! It was the only time his son had understood a situation better than himself. He needn't put that in his account. Oraekja got to Isafjord and equipped a fleet. Snorre fled even further eastwards. Sturla easily won the battle with Oraekja. But he let Oraekja live. At the same time, he ordered his cousin to leave the Westfjords for ever and settle in Stafaholt. That wasn't all. Sturla was to have Reykholt and the whole of its manorial property, and he demanded a lasting peace with Oraekja. Oraekja acquiesced to every one of his demands, not wishing to make the situation even more difficult for his father. Sturla ordered Oraekja to a meeting at Rangarvellir a few days later.

Oraekja was there at the stated time. If the Devil had asked Oraekja to meet him, he would have arrived punctually. His uncle Sighvatr was to meet him. With his seven men, Oraekja awaited his uncle for several hours. No one turned up. It began to get dark. At length, Oraekja rode back the same way he'd come. He had to pick his way carefully in the rugged terrain. He carried a torch in his right hand. He shouted his uncle's name several times. Sometimes he heard the echo of his own voice, sometimes it disappeared into the darkness. Towards midnight, as he was dozing in the saddle, a gang of men stormed out of the darkness and tore him off his rearing horse. He tried to take the torch in his left hand so that he could reach his sword. He was struck on the back of the head, and slipped out of the saddle. After a while, Oraekja got to his feet, dazed.

Sturla was holding the torch. Oraekja's horse was led away. None of his men put up any resistance. Meekly, they allowed their hands to be tied behind their backs, because Oraekja said they should. All night long, Sturla and his men rode with their captives, across hills and bogs, around the arms of fjords, through brush and thicket. Oraekja repeatedly asked where they were going. Sturla didn't answer. In the light from the torches, Oraekja could see how his cousin's face became more and more remote each time he repeated the question. Sometime in the early hours, Orækja stopped asking. The first thing he recognized was a path and then a large boulder, which from his childhood days he'd always imagined to look like a walrus. Orækja was on his way to Reykholt.

It was near this spot that Sturla and Orækja had watched the river in spate, one late spring day when they were boys. The Hvitá had destroyed everything in its head-long rush down the Reykholt valley. Sturla and Orækja had climbed higher up the hillside to count the casualties carried by the floodwaters. As they sat there, a cow came drifting past. It had one brown ear and one white one and large, beautiful eyes. Orækja thought the cow must have been asleep when the flood came. She'd probably felt the water against her ribs and then become frightened as she tried to get back to the barn. She'd have got cramp quite quickly and begun to bellow. The two boys spoke of this with sorrow in their voices as the cow floated past, until she turned, legs uppermost in the water, and vanished with trees and earth and bushes.

By morning, Sturla and Orækja had arrived. The prisoners were pulled off their horses and taken inside Torkild's forge. Sturla told his men to strip the prisoners. With their hands tied behind their backs they were led around the estate. Stones, moss, tools and even food was hurled at them, while insults came thick and fast. The youngest wainwright, who'd known Orækja for many years, tripped him up. Sturla ran and hauled Orækja to his feet with the rope around his wrists. Sturla's cruelty to his cousin did not abate, even though Orækja didn't beg for mercy or cry out. Sturla ordered his men to lead Orækja's seven naked companions around the houses until the sun was at its highest.

'As for Orækja, I'll take him somewhere we both knew well in our youth,' said Sturla. He was speaking so loudly that everyone could hear him. He told two of his men, Svein and Teitur, to come with them. They sat Orækja on his horse. The party left Reykholt with Orækja swaying in the saddle, immediately behind Sturla's white horse. To begin with, Orækja didn't know where they were going. Soon, he knew only too well. He began sweating. When, for a moment, his captors' attention was elsewhere, he threw himself off his horse, head first. Svein hauled him back up again and tied him to the saddle. They were going to Surtshellir. Sturla had threatened to imprison him in that awful cave on several occasions when they'd been children.

As soon as they arrived, and much to Orækja's surprise, Sturla returned to Reykholt alone. Why? Hadn't he'd been looking forward to what was about to happen? As soon as Sturla was out of sight, Orækja was taken from his horse and tied to a post that had been driven into the ground. Orækja just wanted to get it over with. Teitur became uneasy. He asked Orækja if he knew what they were going to do to him. Svein tried to make him keep quiet. Orækja answered that he knew only too well. Teitur was troubled.

'How can you be so calm when you know what's going to happen?' Teitur asked. Then he yelled: 'You're as stupid as a sheep going to slaughter! Why don't you resist?'

Svein hushed him up. Orækja stood erect. He looked dully at Teitur.

'Get on with it,' Orækja said.

'You don't know what *it* is,' Teitur shouted.

'I know everything,' said Orækja. His voice was surprisingly easy.

'Everything?' queried Teitur.

'Yes,' said Orækja. 'Don't you think Sturla is a miserable creature, when he can't even bear to be present?'

Svein hit him in the face. His nose started bleeding.

'We're to tie you! We're to castrate you!' Teitur shouted.

Orækja could see that there were tears in his eyes, before Teitur's fist struck him and he slumped. Svein took out the knife and laid it on the ground. He hauled Orækja into a standing position and bound him even tighter. Svein picked up the knife, grasped Teitur with his other hand and led him some yards away. Svein whispered. Teitur looked down. They were a couple of years younger than him. They were well built and strong. Teitur nodded. There was silence. Their faces assumed a resolute expression. Orækja felt his breath coming faster. The men in front of him ought to know that when they killed him the sun would fall, strike the stars and set them burning before everything went black. Not even night would remain. All would descend with him: the last bird, the last fish, the last human being. He would leave nothing to anyone. He couldn't suppress a scream, loud, unbroken, savage. Birds flew without rhyme or reason, scared out of their nests or tussocks of grass. Sturla was still close enough to hear it. Orækja fainted. After a while, he returned to his senses. They hadn't blinded him! He shouted that he could see. Svein had spared his eyes and only taken one testicle. He gave thanks, to whom he didn't know, that for once he'd had a bit of luck.

There's nothing clever about dying. Surviving is harder. Orækja avoided bleeding to death. Lying across his horse, he was sent back to his wife. Yet again Arnbjørg managed to return him to health. It was the third time she'd saved his life. As soon as he could walk, but before his scars had turned white, he was banished to Norway.

Snorre reached out for his copy of *Heimskringla*. He had managed to write all that in such a short time! What an enterprise, he'd written about every Norwegian king in less than two years. Sæmundr Frodi Sigfusson had written about Norway's kings fifty years before Snorre. He'd studied in Paris. Sæmundr had used exact dates and events, but even he'd had to leave something to guesswork. And wasn't that true of Ari Thorgilsson, too?

Snorre rose, went to the door and opened it. He looked out at the church, as everyone did, it resembled a shield. The church explained everything. The church stood where it always stood. It was dusk. The air had turned cooler.

Perhaps he should talk to Arnbjørn about evil? Although Iceland's dominant families had taken all the power and property into their own hands and ought to have had more than enough of everything, they constantly waged civil war. A couple of days earlier, Snorre had watched some children kick a puppy until it lay lifeless on the ground. Was O><ækja the Devil incarnate? And what about him, who so often needed O><ækja's services? Would Arnbjørn say that God is willing to prevent evil but isn't able to? Or the reverse, that he could but doesn't want to? No, he couldn't talk to the priest about such things. He closed the door carefully behind him and sat down at the desk.

Snorre's brother Thordr had told him that Sturla wanted to write the Sturlungs' saga. Could he trust him? Nobody could be trusted these days. Sturla was dangerously good with words. He really must make a start. He allowed his eyes to rest on the objects on his desk. A coconut he'd bought from an Egyptian merchant during a visit to Skåne. A thorn from Jesus' crown, which had been sent by a monastery outside Paris. A tiny piece of the tablecloth that had been used by Jesus and his Disciples at the Last Supper, which he'd inherited from Jon Loptsson who had, in turn, got it from Constantinople. His greatest treasure, however, was a small blue bottle that stood right in front of him. There was water in the bottle. Holy water from Sul in Verdal, Trøndelag. The spring from which St Olav had drunk. His wives had poked fun at his eagerness to collect objects of all kinds. To avoid their sniping, he'd laid many lovely things aside. But nobody could touch these. Soon, it would be quite dark. Was that a noise he heard? He put down his pen. He ought to eat something. He lay forward and let his head rest on the desk. The last thought he had before dropping off to sleep was that Orækja would have to help him. If not, he might never see her again. It was that bad! Snorre would have to beg help from his son, the son who believed that the thrust of a sword was more useful than any word. Now, to see his love again, he was dependent on Orækja. How helpless he'd become!

Two of Gissur Thorvaldsson's men crept across the yard. They'd been there before. They listened at his door for a long time. Then, one of them opened the door, almost silently. Snorre was snoring with his head turned to the door. The man closed it carefully. They weren't to touch him, but just to find out if Snorre slept in the same place, and make certain that he was alone.

'Orækja!' cried the sleeper within.

21 SEPTEMBER
1241

Snorre sat up. It must be the middle of the night, the room was dim.

The seventy men who rode towards Reykholt under the command of Gissur Thorvaldsson derived a strength and resourcefulness from their thirst for revenge that Snorre could have done with.

Outside, he could see two stars. The tallow candle by his side had almost burnt out. In his sleep, he'd upset the candle stand over the inkwell. He managed to right the stand before the flame expired. The tallow from the candle must on no account be allowed to run into the ink.

When he rose, he could glimpse the books that still remained to him after the distribution of Hallveig's estate. Some weeks before, her sons Klængr and Ormr had taken more than half the books and the best part of the furnishings. He had hoped they'd leave him in peace after his considerable generosity in sharing out the furniture. The tactic hadn't worked. The brothers had ridden up a couple of days after their mother's interment. They had demanded half the estate! Ormr was the one who did the talking. The brothers recalled only too well how little Snorre had grieved when their father, Bjørn Thorvaldsson, had died more than a decade before. Instead of emphasizing how unreasonable their demand was, he had plied them with food and drink and attempted to smile and laugh whenever he could. He shared out books, candlesticks, rugs and wall hangings so liberally that even Klængr was heard to mumble words of thanks. He hoped that the brothers would be satisfied with that and set off for home as soon as possible.

'Well, it's good that Reykholt's chattels have been divided up,' said Ormr. 'Now we can make a start on things of real value.' Snorre tried to look doubtful in an artless way. The brothers wanted the farms Bláskógaheidi, Reykholt and Stafaholt to be divided immediately. The houses and property around them were worth a lot in themselves but, in addition, the farms were also rich church lands. The owner had the right to demand his share of the tithe from the peasants and bondsmen who lived in the fief. As for Bessastadir, Snorre argued that there was nothing to discuss. He'd bought that entirely with his own money. Ormr forced a crooked smile and said that they hadn't said anything about Bessastadir. The three other properties were the only ones that had been mentioned. Snorre gave them more books without getting anything in return. On the contrary, they had mounted their horses, with the books and the rest of the things in carts, and shouted that they wouldn't give up. They rode to the farm of Bær, parked the carts and galloped to their uncle, Gissur Thorvaldsson, to ask for help. That was all the thanks he received.

By the light of the tiny flame that still hovered above the wick, he made out the shapes of the five books he had left. No matter what posterity would say about the things he'd written, whether good or bad, it would at least be better than the life he'd lived. Millions of letters, painstakingly written on calfskin, with gold and silver illumination, had been handed over by him to that couple of greedy louts. Could they read? There wasn't much in their manner that suggested it. But the brothers knew how easy it would be to sell the beautiful books to churches, monasteries and noblemen in England and Norway.

But what did they know about the work that lay behind each book? Not to mention the intellectual power that drove the quill's nib over the calfskin. If you looked at the individual page, it resembled a tundra. Using a lime solution he'd managed to clean off fat, hair and remnants of flesh, before stretching the skin on a frame, then thoroughly scraping it, rubbing in chalk and smoothing it out with a pumice stone. He could hear his raw material bellowing outside. What skin! It took the ink so well. And if you made a mistake, it could be scraped or washed away. *Heim-skringla* and the *Younger Edda* had been dictated. Now he would write himself. Tomorrow morning, in the first light of dawn, he would begin at last. Now he must douse the light and get to bed. But he mustn't forget to eat first. Had it been hunger that had awoken him? He bent and opened the small cupboard by the side of his bed. His hand fumbled in the semi-darkness until it found the half-eaten wheat loaf. He grasped it and fed it into his mouth. He chewed as he walked back, doused the candle and climbed into bed.

The priest would doubtless be preparing for the Feast of St Maurice. That was why he hadn't seen him recently. Why worry himself? Arnbjørn wanted to be on his own to improve his sermon. That was hardly surprising. He had himself suggested, when Arnbjørn sought his advice, that the priest should vary his sermons more.

He got out of bed, seated himself at his desk and lit the candle. He tried once again to put down a few sentences. He couldn't. Was this the end? Couldn't he write any more? It was hopeless. This was his last attempt at writing.

Snorre banged his fist on the desk. He was too tired, it was as simple as that. He blew out the candle and went to bed. He lay beneath the large rug with its red-and-blue snake motif. The house was no longer lit by the two stars. Sleep slowly closed his eyes, and he began to dream.

He was lying in the middle of the yard at Reykholt. He tried to raise his left leg. Nothing happened. He checked to see if the swollen ankle obeyed him. It lay immobile. Then he repeated the same routine with his right leg. Perhaps the toes could move? They were motionless. The sun stared down at him. He tried to close his eyes. They didn't want to. He was lying in the centre of the yard in front of the main house, under the clouds that didn't move, under all that blueness, under the sun's staring eye. He wanted to shout—Here I am!—loud and clear so that everyone at Reykholt could hear him. They would hear the force in his voice, just as they had heard it for years, the great chieftain, the skald, the clear voice of the master. His mouth would not open. There were people. Why hadn't he noticed them? He knew each one. Arnbjørn, Kyrre, Gyda, the young lad who helped Kyrre and Torkild! Snorre tried to yell at the top of his voice. No one heard him. His brothers arrived. After a while, Orækja and Margrete came. Orækja was weeping. Margrete was holding her hand in front of her eyes. Her mouth was open. A hole. He heard nothing. What were they doing? The people of Reykholt had formed a circle around him. They began to move! Torkild left the circle. He bent down in front of him and looked into his face. A man was crouching immediately behind his head. That must be Kyrre. They picked him up. Now he could see even more of them. Margrete and Orækja both stood with bowed heads. He was lowered to the ground again. Kyrre tried to close his eyes. His eyelids slipped open again. He was lifted and lowered gently into the ground. He found himself below

the level of the earth. He could see them up there. He tried
to scream. They clustered round the hole above him. It was
just large enough for his body. Their faces became darker,
they were blocking out the sun. Arnbjørn the priest was
the only one who raised his arms. His lips moved. He made
the sign of the cross. Three of the men left the circle. They
returned, each carrying a rake. The earth around the grave
fell heavily over his calves and thighs. His brother Thordr
shovelled earth and sand over his hips and stomach. Was
that Margrete he could hear wailing? Had he felt Orækja's
tears falling on him? He glimpsed the hand of the priest
raised towards heaven. Earth, sand and stones covered him.
He heard every single word. Even the whispers came to his
ears. The crying, the sobbing. The words of Arnbjørn the
priest, Thordr's sigh of relief, Gyda's tears, Orækja's hopeless
laments, Torkild's remark to Kyrre that there was something
they needed to discuss later. And as if that weren't enough,
the bishop's voice was one of the chorus. There! Even the
bishop had bestirred himself. And, of course, Ormr and
Klængr. Now was the moment to push Orækja off balance,
goad him into losing control, drawing his sword, going
berserk, so that the Althing would sentence him to forfeit
his inheritance rights. After blackness had descended on
him, they were making their plans. Ormr was telling Klængr
how much Orækja was whining, in all his distracted sorrow
and helplessness, on the opposite side of the grave. What
would the wild man get up to, now that his father lay under
the sod? He could tell Ormr was smiling by the sound of
his breathing. And that was Gissur's voice, he heard it clearly.
What was he doing here? Just as he was about to recognize
one of the new voices that had arrived, he shot down into
the earth. He had no idea how long this breakneck journey
lasted, but his subterranean travels ended as abruptly as

they'd begun. He was lying by the side of a rock. He was in what looked like a huge cave. Where was it? In the cave he found a small tarn. The cave had four openings. He walked further into the largest tunnel that led off from the main cave. He'd been here before. At the far end, he saw some high columns of ice that reached from floor to ceiling. Snorre turned and walked cautiously in the opposite direction. In the front part of the cave, he found three side caves. What was that he could hear? Ear-splitting screams. He recognized the voice. He trampled on some bones. In between each scream he could hear cursing and whimpering. It was Orækja's voice. Two unknown men stood in front of Orækja. His body was firmly bound with a thick rope. One man was holding his unfettered arms. The other was stabbing him. Now he knew where he was. They were inside Surtshellir, where, with his own eyes, he'd seen criminals and murderers incarcerated. Warily, Snorre moved away from Orækja and the two men. The cries receded. He increased his pace towards the exit. The light around him grew a little. He managed to walk even faster. Snorre tried to block his ears. At last, he could see the opening. The rays of daylight reached into the cave like taut lifelines. The cries got closer again. He crawled up the final steep slope and then he was out in the blessed light. The screams ceased. He was breathing heavily. He glanced down at his boots. Blood from Orækja's wounds had covered the leather. He lifted his foot. There were shining grains on the sole of his boot. He'd heard stories of this happening to other people too, but he hadn't believed them. There was gold sand beneath his feet. Carefully, he removed his boots and laid them soles up. He knelt and gently swept each golden grain into his cupped, expectant hand. When all had been gathered up, he raised his eyes to Sleipnir, who was waiting for him. The glint of gold was in Sleipnir's eyes. It shone so brightly that Snorre blinked several times. Something like a smile spread across what had once been his face. But what had happened to Sleipnir? His forehead, cheeks, muzzle, temples, throat, neck, chest, mane, back, flanks, coat and belly were just as before, but his legs? Sleipnir now had eight legs, just like the Sleipnir of Odin and Freyja. It must have happened whilst he was in the cave. Sleipnir stared at the gold in Snorre's hand. His gaze never wavered. And his penis? It straightened with vernal power until it hit the ground with a gentle thud. A little gust of wind blew over the two of them. He didn't close his hand in time. The gold dust was swept off his palm. He ran after it until he was standing near the water's edge in inky darkness.

'Is there nothing I can do?' Snorre asked.

'Wake up,' a voice answered.

And he did.

The sound was still in the room as he sat up in bed.

'Wake up,' he repeated more softly.

He climbed out of bed, stood erect for a second, sat down and put his shoes on. He went to the long table, leant on it and assured himself that his chase after the gold dust from Surtshellir was just a dream. Why had he dreamt about Sleipnir? Margrete's words came back to his mind:

'Take care of that little horse of yours.'

Dreaming of horses was a bad omen. It was superstition, of course. He had never doubted it. Even so, an unpleasant lingering qualm remained. It would have been best if he hadn't dreamt at all. The old were troubled by such thoughts. His body, certainly, was no longer as young as it had been. But his mind, that was young. Even though Margrete had questioned the fact after their meeting with Knut Storskald at the Althing. Perhaps it was simply that he liked thinking of himself as young in spirit? It was morning outside. What had become of the people on the estate? What was the matter with them?

He would try to sit at his desk for most of the day. Orækja wasn't around, but the words still wouldn't come together properly. It was obviously no use. The previous evening, the words had seemed like a rib here, a board there, a couple of nails here, a block and tackle there. He couldn't put them together to form a keel and a hull that would float, and make the sentence sail. He'd end up going to Mauricemas. As soon as Mass was over, he could speak to Arnbjørn. Now he simply had to confide the anxieties he felt.

What was the weather like? Carefully, he opened the door a crack and peered out. The sky was high and cloudless. It would be a couple of months before snow would fall gently on Reykholt. A few fat flakes would dissolve on the ground, revealing themselves to be raindrops in disguise. Then, a whole host of white petal flakes would drift, light and merry, through the air. They would fall and fall, but even so they would fly a bit before they fell. Some of them would even begin to rise again before falling, slowly at first, then a bit faster, until they landed on the corner of the church tower. After a tiny rest, some of them would end their journey on the hairy, off-white coat of an unsuspecting horse. Other flakes were aiming for the main house, but would change course at the last moment and end up in the open, blood-red mouth of a child with its tongue sticking out. Most of the snowflakes would land on an already heavily laden cart making for the gate to the field outside the ramparts. A somewhat foreshortened covering of snow would settle on most of the roofs. And after a little while one would notice how the sound of voices, footsteps, wheels and whetstones had been muffled by all this whiteness. Even the subterranean chuckling of the hot spring to Snorre's Bath would get fainter and fainter, as if running slowly along a slim arm in which the blood was thinking of turning to ice.

What a fool he'd been! He'd driven Orækja away from him. He needed to keep his son under his thumb. Now there was a risk he'd never come back. It put Snorre in mind of a big farmer he knew who'd wanted to set his bondsman free. The bondsman had implored the farmer not to do it. The farmer thought the bondsman was making fun of him. But when he gave the bondsman his liberty, the bondsman killed him.

He'd never understood Orækja. When Orækja was a boy, only about eight years old, Snorre had found him lying motionless on his stomach with his face in the heather. When asked why he was lying like that, the boy had said that he was looking down into the past. Boys didn't say that sort of thing. Snorre shook his head. He'd felt neither joy nor pride over this strange statement. Merely uneasiness.

Three days before, Orækja had said he'd returned to Reykholt to do some hawking. That was clearly an excuse. The real reason was to find out how things stood with his father. Snorre had just told him to leave. He'd been uncompromising. Heartless and mean. A manner reserved for traitors and enemies. This was his own son, the man he needed more than anyone to help him cling on to the remnants of his power and property. Orækja, he called aloud across the open space in front of him, then he fell silent. He began walking quickly towards the south gate. Perhaps he wasn't far away? He must be there! Snorre mumbled, 'Please come back, dear son. I need you. Understand that.'

God had decided to destroy Sodom and Gomorrah. Lot, who lived at Sodom, was visited by angels. 'Flee for your lives; do not look back and do not stop anywhere in the Plain,' they said. As soon as Lot's family had left the city, God rained down fire and brimstone on Sodom. All life was expunged. Lot's wife stopped while they were fleeing, she turned round and looked at the destruction. She was transformed into a pillar of salt. Why did she turn? Out of compassion? To search for her sons-in-law who had stayed behind? Did God punish her with such severity because she had been a witness to his vengefulness?

Snorre walked faster. He was breathing heavily. A smell that he didn't at first recognize assailed his nostrils. He raised his head. Who had opened the gate? Had Orækja returned? He tried to walk even more quickly. If it was Orækja, he would forgive him everything. Everything. He stood at the gate a long time. There was no one in sight. Was there anyone outside the ramparts he couldn't see? For a great while, he stared at the ridges, the hills and the mountains in the distance that blocked out the sea. His eyes strayed to the enclosure beyond the ramparts. He must try to calm down. Kyrre had sought permission to enclose the three mares with their foals. The stallions had been so restless recently that it had affected the foals. The grass had been grazed right down. Instead of moving the enclosure, Kyrre's boy had heaved a haycock over the fence. It irritated Snorre that they'd begun to use the winter hay.

This wasn't the first time he'd experienced the apathy of his workers. It never crossed their minds that it might be expensive or cause problems later on. What if there was a drought and a long winter to follow? It didn't matter to Kyrre because they weren't his horses. But Kyrre *was* interested in earning easy money! He fed the mares and foals with the best hay because he couldn't be bothered to move the fence posts. That was the way of it.

The foals in the enclosure were the same colour as their mothers. He couldn't remember anything like that ever happening before. One or two, but never three mares with foals the same colour at the same time. Kyrre's helper was also looking at the horses. He pretended not to see Snorre. The biggest mare was grey. The other two were black and brown. The horses were bigger than Sleipnir. They'd been bought in Norway the year before.

They had a definite pecking order. Sleipnir would never have submitted to it. Snorre was proud of the fact. The brown mare was eating the hay. The others remained at a respectful distance. The mares kept close to their foals. The brown foal was clearly replete, it nudged the forelegs of its still chewing mother. She continued eating for a while. The grey mare whinnied in the background. Her foal repeated the whinny a little more softly, but the shake of the head was the same. The brown mare and foal stepped quickly back. The black mare and foal moved even further away. The brown mare paused in her eating. The grey approached the hay. As soon as the brown noticed this, she flattened her ears, neighed, turned her head to one side and showed her teeth. The brown foal ran towards the grey foal. This made the greys move towards the blacks. Not next to them but in front. Only when the brown mare and foal had moved completely away from the hay, was it time. Less than half remained. The greys advanced with cautious steps. Was anything more soothing to the mind than watching hoses?

Of course he could relax without sitting in the pool.

He glanced at the gate. What was that smell he'd caught on the other side of it? A gust of wind made him fancy he recognized the smell. The odour was heavy and slightly sweet. The smell of the hay and the horses made him look at the grey mare again. She finished eating quickly but the foal chewed slowly. The black mare came too close. The grey bridled and then placed her hindquarters by the foal's working mouth and whisked away impertinent flies. After the foal had eaten its fill, the greys moved away, and the blacks finally got their turn. The straws that were left could have been counted on the fingers of both hands. They had all eaten one after the other. The black horse was left standing alone. Suddenly, she began to quiver and run, without any object and with a limitless freedom that was just as empty in one direction as in the other, until she stood bewildered and allowed herself to be tempted by Kyrre's boy with a handful of hay. Sleipnir would never have behaved like that. Sleipnir was never at anyone's beck and call.

There was that smell again.

If only Orækja would come! He would thank him now. Praise him in many words, with witnesses present. Had he ever said anything nice to him? He went back through the gate and shut it. He'd been petty and ungrateful. He'd made the same mistake as when Little Jon had wanted to marry and asked for a reasonable dowry. Orækja had never asked for anything at all.

Now he knew what it was.

It couldn't be Orækja who was behind this! His eyes glistened with tears. He turned his steps towards the pool. He'd harboured so many nights' bad dreams against his son!

It was *there* the smell was coming from. The sight made him cry, he sobbed and talked incoherently between his gasps. He clenched his fists. Water was continually feeding the pool, and instantly turning red. He wiped away tears with his hand. He looked about him. The stench of blood forced its way into his nostrils, his mouth and his throat. He came to a halt a couple of yards from the pool. He trembled. He stopped crying. There were no more words. His mouth was open. Around his eyes and nose the skin was grimy with tears.

His cry lasted long enough for those whom it shook from sleep to register that it came from a grown man. A loud, piercing cry arose from the pool, reverberated all around the steading and pulled a piece of heaven down over the old man. A stake had been driven deep into the ground next to the pool. There were gory footprints on the ground. Blood was still dripping from the stake. The blood ran from the stone slab next to the stake and into the grass and the earth. The horse's eyes were open, his mouth half open. The stake was leaning towards Snorre. The head it was supporting was heavy enough to make it tip gently forwards. He was standing before Sleipnir's head. He screamed out Orækja's name. The fractured neck vertebra protruded. The throat had been cut. He studied Sleipnir's large, brown, expressionless eyes, which had ranged so far and wide. He couldn't remember ever having seen fear in those eyes. The way he'd moved, his neighing, with his ears out to the sides, his stamping hooves, all these had of course sometimes displayed restlessness. But Snorre had never seen fear in him. He put his right hand on Sleipnir's brow. With his left, he dried his face.

'Whoa,' said Snorre.

Gently, he stroked the horse's mouth. It was almost cold. His forelock hung there as if nothing had happened. He turned his eyes hesitantly to the pool. A little movement in the wind caused Sleipnir's forelock to stir.

He looked down at the pool. The back legs straddled its edge. Flesh and sinew had begun to loosen at the place where head and neck had divided from the rest of the body. The sand-coloured stones were dark with blood. The pool was cloudy. Who could have thought of raising this totem against him? They must know him well. Had Klængr and Ormr won Orækja over to their side?

Most of the people on the estate were scared of Orækja. Both Kyrre and Torkild had gained some credibility by telling Orækja how much Snorre hated him. It is impossible to exaggerate the baseness of mankind. If they could tell tales about their master to a man they really feared, they took the first opportunity to do so. That was the way of things. If they did the Devil a service, they were certain to get something in return. If the news was important enough and the effect of the gossip poisonous enough, they could expect the service to be reciprocated. As if the Devil kept his bargains!

Snorre began to berate himself for not speaking peacefully to his son the last time they met at the pool. He should have been grateful for that pleasant day and night he'd spent at his nephew Tumi's the week before. It had certainly been very agreeable. With Tumi, he had discussed what they should do to accommodate Ormr and Klængr regarding Hallveig's estate.

The same evening Snorre arrived at the farm, Tumi sent two of his men to find Orækja and Sturla Thorvaldsson and get them to come as quickly as possible to Saudafjell.

By the very next evening they were present to assess the situation together. Not only had he learnt that he was over-estimating the brothers' vindictiveness, but also that most of his family was behind him. Surely he couldn't deny that his own son and Sturla and his host, too, were men of action? They hadn't managed to convince him. But what had put him in a good mood was the way Oraekja had been accepted by the others. He had clasped his son for a moment and asked if he'd like to arm wrestle, just as they'd done when Oraekja was a boy. Laughing, father and son had arm wrestled, to the great delight of the others. The atmosphere was hardly dampened when Tumi said that he'd got a large consignment of German beer in the house. The beer had come from a merchantman that had sailed from Bremen. Beer certainly wasn't the only thing aboard. Casks of red wine, honey and spices they'd never seen before were all set before them. This was all served after they'd eaten large amounts of roast lamb. At the end, they'd been given cored apples in honey syrup. During this last course they'd drunk a sweet, yellow wine he'd never tasted before. He didn't mention this to anyone. It was his host who noticed Snorre's look of surprise after taking the first sip from his silver goblet. Tumi asked if he liked the wine. Snorre nodded and immediately drained the goblet. After the red wine and the sweet wine were finished, they drank beer.

It had been a long time since he'd felt so easy with other members of his family. It was only later in the evening that he remembered the letter he'd received some days earlier. A man in his position had to expect unkind comments. He'd got used to that, but this was clearly a death-threat, written in a semi-literate hand. The writing looked like imitation runes.

An Althing representative who'd formerly stood for Sæmundr Jonsson of Oddi had forwarded the letter. Snorre had read it time and again. He didn't understand much of it, apart from the maliciousness of its tone. Orækja's name was mentioned in strong terms. He drew his host aside and showed the letter to him. Why did he want to spoil a good party, his host asked, and cast a quick eye over the letter, shrugged his shoulders and advised him to forget it and keep it hidden from his son. Why should Snorre trouble himself over a letter that hadn't even been signed by its sender? Someone with power and authority wouldn't have hesitated to sign. Snorre pushed it inside his shirt and said he'd think no more about it. Maybe Tumi or Sturla had told Orækja about it after he'd left?

The letter had in fact been penned by an abject man who'd been paid to write it by Snorre's killer. Two days later, the author would look on Snorre's corpse and boast that the letter was his.

The following morning, Orækja and Sturla had ridden part of the way to Reykholt with Snorre, before he continued alone. He sat on Sleipnir and closed first one eye and then the other. He sat thinking that death might be quite an experience if, now and again, you could open an eye. He encountered no one on the path home that afternoon in early September, 1241.

Snorre dried his tears on his arm as he stretched his hand towards Sleipnir's forelock. He rubbed the thick hair between his fingers. He was no longer aware of the stench of blood. He thought of Margete and whether her husband might be behind this. Had Egil married Margrete out of pure spite so that everyone else, and particularly he, Snorre, would be denied the opportunity? He whispered the words into Sleipnir's ear.

Snorre heard bleating far away. Hadn't Kyrre managed to chase the sheep away from Reykholt yet? He looked around. A flock of more than a score were approaching beyond the ramparts. Who'd implanted the idea in them that there was any grass left so close to the houses? They had no business here. Since early morning, they'd grazed with their mouths in the shade of their bodies. They jostled one another, bleated, jostled one another again, bleated and shook their heads. They bleated to remind themselves that they were alive. Their steps were so tiny they were like old men walking on polished ice. The rays of the sun struck into the sheep's wool, where they would glow all day long.

Outside the ramparts, in the opposite direction, two men approached carrying a rope. Snorre didn't notice them. They kept to the paths to avoid making unnecessary noise. They had fastened their swords to their backs, the way they carried their quivers. The men moved fast but didn't run. At the closed gate, they sent each other a look, leaned close to the woodwork, nodded to each other and moved a few yards off.

Snorre turned away from Sleipnir's head and the pool. With slow steps he made his way towards the houses. His heart beat. His skeleton kept him erect. His soles were worn. He didn't fall. He walked on. He didn't clasp his hands. They hung down, swinging gently backwards and forwards. He stared straight ahead.

Torkild stood outside the ramparts holding the coil of rope. The other man, dark-haired and compact, with a short, agile body, tied a noose at one end of it. He deftly lassoed a post that stuck out of the palisade on top of the ramparts. It was done almost noiselessly. The rope was pulled tight. They waited a few seconds, listened, glanced at each other and pointed. The rope reached straight up the rampart and palisade, then formed an angle at the top of the fence before encompassing the thick post. The dark-haired man took a good grip of the rope with both hands and climbed the vertical rampart. Once at the top, he looked in the direction of the houses first. There was no one to be seen. He was just about to whisper to Torkild to follow him. When he caught sight of Snorre his heart amost stopped. He gulped but noticed that his breath came more easily after watching the old man's gait. Snorre was alone. Although a cat was trying to rub against the leg of Reykholt's master, he didn't appear to notice it. Come right on up! He jumped over the palisade at the top of the rampart. Once they were both on top, they loosened the knot and pulled the rope off the post.

As soon as Snorre passed the forge and disappeared from view, the dark-haired man leapt down. He landed on his feet, turned and reached for the coil of rope that was thrown after him. The big man jumped after him, fell but found his feet again at once. Snorre walked slowly towards the church. They went towards the gate. They opened it wide. Using their swords, they levered off the planks that were used to bar it. To keep the gate open, they lashed it to two stout beams sticking out of the rampart. They exchanged glances. The dark-haired man asked his companion why he hated Snorre. He was the one who'd identified Sleipnir amongst the horses. He was the one who knew the layout of the houses in detail and Snorre's routine and habits. It was he who'd willingly offered to serve Snorre's greatest enemy. Without preamble, he explained that Snorre had seduced his young wife a couple of years before. When he'd found out about it, his wife had fled from Reykholt. He'd never seen her again.

Torkild had already asked his new master, his eyes expressionless, if he could go in to Snorre alone and strike the first blow.

They both directed their gaze to Snorre, who was climbing the steps to the church door. He panted heavily on the top one. Snorre looked down at his clothes, straightened them and attempted to open the door. It wouldn't budge. He tried again. The door wouldn't open. The two men could hear him shout: 'Open up! I know you're there, Priest Arnbjørn!'

They looked at one another. They knew where the priest was. They were ready to run out of the gate and warn the others outside.

'Arnbjørn, I've got to speak to you! Something terrible's happened. Where is everyone? Help me!'

Snorre knocked even louder, then waited a moment before turning, descending the steps and going to his house.

'The big fish is ready for cooking now,' Torkild said, before they began to run.

The great September moon already hung red and round above the yard. Long shadows stretched right up to the house wall. Snorre stepped over the shadow that fell on the flagstones in front of the door. He must get to bed. He was exhausted. His face was still grimy with tears. It was possible to make out the lines around his eyes. They were moist, with a grey jellyfish at their centre. His lips were dry, his body shook. For the first time he noticed that his hands had become bonier. His wrists and finger joints were more wrinkled than he remembered them. He fell onto his bed with his clothes on. His mouth managed to open in a yawn before he fell asleep.

It was in the time of the angels, before all dreams had to be understood. Snorre saw the angel quite clearly as he lay in bed, snoring heavily. As soon as the angel entered the room, it took up position by the foot of the bed. His legs were so swollen that he hadn't been able to get his boots off. He sat up. The angel, in Margrete's shape, retreated to a corner of the twilit room. It wasn't the first time he'd had this dream. Each time it became more detailed. The previous year, Margrete had levelled an accusation against him that he wasn't able to refute. He pretended he hadn't been affected by it. From its corner, the angel looked at him. He felt the piercing gaze. His heart muscles were so rapidly filled with fresh blood that he felt the tug at his chest. Each time he thought he was embracing her, she turned into a golden light, and her feathers got smaller and smaller as he clutched her. Finally, they became hard and grey, and the angel had changed into a hunting falcon.

It had all begun so peacefully, late one evening, a year ago. Margrete and Snorre were at last able to spend a day and night together on a farm, overlooking the monastery on the island of Videy. Never in his most melancholy moods could he have imagined that the evening would develop into a long argument and an indictment she would never retract.

Two years before Margrete married and had her first child, she'd been on a pilgrimage to Rome. Several people Snorre knew, both family and friends, had been to the Pope's City. After sailing to the Continent, they took the road to Paris. From there, the journey continued to Lucca for a sight of the Volto Santo crucifix. When the holy Nicodemus in Palestine tried to fashion the face on the crucifix, he was assisted by the Holy Ghost himself. The crucifix had helped thousands of people with fertility problems, Margrete amongst them.

Snorre had seen large parts of Norway and southern Sweden, but he'd never been to Rome. He couldn't travel too far from Reykholt and Iceland. What would Oraekja get up to while he was away in Rome? It was just impossible. He had to take care of his property and what was left of his clan and country.

In dulcet tones, Margrete had begun by asking him if he liked the vase she'd given him depicting the lovers, Hero and Leander. She had bought the vase in Rome from a Franciscan monk who'd fled Constantinople in 1204. Snorre pretended he didn't know anything about the myth of Hero and Leander. She eagerly narrated the story of Hero's father who kept her locked up in a tower on a small island off Constantinople, so Leander couldn't meet her. But every night, she climbed to the top of the tower with a torch, and that gave him something to swim towards. Night after night they held their secret trysts. One stormy night the torch blew out. Next morning, she found him drowned. Instead of pulling him ashore, Hero threw herself into the water to be united with her lover.

'Would you have done what Hero did?' she asked.

'Yes,' he replied without hesitation.

She looked into his eyes. His answer had been a bit too pat.

'Are you sure?'

'I think so,' he said hesitantly.

'Can I trust you?' The atmosphere was strained. She didn't give him time to reply.

'Let's talk instead about the two cities you'd like to visit—Rome and Constantinople.'

'Yes,' he said with relief, as if she'd rescued him from an ambush. He'd never met anyone who could talk so readily about cities and places, apart from Jon Loptsson. When she spoke, it was as if they'd been transported there together. He didn't notice the undertone in her voice. He could see every detail as she talked, he heard the gossip, the scandal, the prayers and the consternation at the prices the egg-sellers were demanding. She brought to life the blind beggars in Rome who reached out imploring hands and who, in the afternoons, regained their sight and did other kinds of work.

It was she who described to him water spurting in all directions, from spouts fat and thin, that raised themselves in arcs and played in the sunshine. It was she who made him see the fine foam that became a mist. Enthralled by her voice, he could hear melodic splashing. He'd never seen a fountain. Suddenly, her voice assumed a sharper note.

'Even though this is the city where the archbishop of Lund and Nidaros was consecrated, it's also the city that executed the apostles Peter and Paul,' she said. 'Peter was crucified by Nero, but Paul was a Roman citizen and it was against the law to subject him to torture. He was beheaded. Today, white lilies bob at the spot where his head was severed from his body. Rome is the city that honoured Nero and built its Colosseum on the bed of the lake in the emperor's park, and, over the centuries, allowed thousands upon thousands of people and animals to be slaughtered to the rapturous delight of the spectators. It is in this city that the pope wishes to live.'

Instead of letting her finish, he asked, 'What exactly are you driving at?'

'I asked if I could trust you. Don't tell me you didn't know what happened in 1204. You were twenty-six at the time. If you didn't know about it then, you were certainly aware of it by the time you wrote *Heimskringla*.'

As soon as Margrete arrived in Rome, she had asked to see as many relics as possible. She wanted to see the crown of thorns, pieces of Christ's cross and the nails. The Franciscan monk told her that most of the relics had come from Constantinople. Emperor Constantine's mother, Helena, had had most of the relics shipped from Jerusalem to Constantinople eight hundred years earlier. Rome had next to nothing. All the relics that had been in the Hagia Sophia and other churches in Constantinople were either burnt or stolen. Not by infidels but by the Crusaders from Rome and Venice, the Normans and the Franks. In Rome, Margrete had met the offspring of refugees, who had only just escaped the arrows, swords and flames. After an exhausting journey around the Mediterranean by donkey, horse and on foot, via Pristina, Dubrovnik, Trieste and Venice and thence to Rome, they learnt that it was the pope himself who had blessed the Venetian fleet and the army that took part in the massacre of their Christian brothers in Constantinople.

Having enjoyed an alliance with Byzantium and Constantinople throughout three Crusades, the pope relegated them to the status of infidels because they permitted various faiths to be practised within the city. The leading Venetian families wanted a monopoly of trade with this enormous empire. Constantinople was the sun in the Byzantine sky— the empire stretched from the walls of Genoa and Ravenna to Athens and Sparta, from the coast of North Africa to the Tigris and the Sinai Desert. No one had ever seen a wealthier or more powerful city than Constantinople. It was ransacked

of everything. She had seen some of the loot herself in
Venice and Rome. All the jewels and gold in the crucifixes
and icons were stolen. Peace be upon Him. In Hagia Sophia
itself, the biggest church in the world, they pillaged while
priests and monks bled to death in the sacristy!

'And you've heard nothing of all this? I ask if I can
trust you. You don't answer, Snorre! Why have you kept
silent about this betrayal and the murders of those who
showed mercy in Constantinople? Is the history you write
just for popes and Mammon?' She added quietly, 'You
could be the victim of some great act of treachery too.'

They didn't share a bed that night.

The following morning, they hadn't had much to say
to each other. They walked slowly side by side along the
shore, with its view over the water to the monastery on
Videy. He threw stones in the water. She looked at the
ground. Suddenly she kissed him, a long and passionate
kiss. He returned the kiss, a little more diffidently. She
loosened his belt and quickly pulled his breeches down.

'Monks might be passing by,' Snorre said.

She took his hands and sat on her haunches. He followed her example. She laid him gently on the shingle. He
let it happen. He could feel every pebble in his back, hips
and thighs. He stared into her face. Her cheeks were flaming
red. She raised her skirt and sat astride him.

He recalled that her eyes had been moist.

Snorre coughed and sat up in bed. He went over to
the table, took the half-full cup of broth left over from the
evening before, set it on the still hot embers for a moment
before lifting it to his lips. His movements were slow and
hesitant. He wasn't fully awake. He thought of the stone
building, the green grass, the horses, Jon Loptsson's slightly

hunched back, the industrious workers at Oddi—especially clear was Gyda, who found the finest feathers for quills. He took a couple of mouthfuls and lay down, closed his eyes for a long sleep. He smiled, quite unable to explain the true source of his joy. He wanted to return to sleep, to the state he didn't want to relinquish, he wanted to remain there for the rest of his life.

The man with only a few hours left to live stared up at the ceiling for a long while, before he eventually fell asleep again.

Not far away, Gissur Thorvaldsson learnt from Torkild that Sleipnir had been butchered as arranged. Torkild asked if he should do the same with Margrete. Gissur shook his head and told Torkild that his vengefulness was making him blind. Torkild must hold himself in check, or keep out of the way.

'Within a day Snorre will be dead, and you won't have a hand in his killing. You're not detached enough. But you're a good scout. Farewell,' said Gissur, turning on his heel and going to speak to his other men. It was an hour before midnight.

22 SEPTEMBER
1241

The time was ripe, and the gate was open. They didn't want to meet any resistance. At midnight, they advanced. Not just one or two but seventy men, all armed. They came on horseback and on foot. Ten men were kept on guard outside the ramparts. Two of them stationed themselves at the open south gate, and two at the north. Six of them were mounted. They rode between the two gates of Reykholt, three on the west side and three on the east, to take care of any attempt at escape. Their patrolling was unnecessary. The other sixty men formed a ring inside the ramparts.

The ultimate and most common conceit is to discover, far too late, that death will come to you too. Snorre would never experience the gradual breaking of dawn over Reykholt.

He tossed and turned in bed. He woke at about three o'clock and paced the floor restlessly. He lay down again. What was he to do? His body turned on to its left side. He stretched out his legs beneath the covers. Only now did Snorre realize that he would never manage to complete a single page about himself and his times. Just imagine those unpolished sentences falling into the hands of the wrong people.

Snorre lit the candle and set fire to his words before dousing the light. Had he said it clearly enough to her? He loved her. What should he do? He got back into bed. He had to see her. He pushed his right hand under his head.

She must be in no doubt about what he felt. Poor Orækja!
He had his unruly side, of course. But he meant well. Who
hasn't made mistakes? Didn't Moses kill more than once?
David sent his servant to war. God even foregave St Olav his
most turbulent years, before he was saved and able to show
mercy himself. And what of Harald Hardråde? Even though
he was a competent poet, a crueller king would have been
hard to find. But he, too, could show goodness. And his own
conduct was hardly of the best, for that matter.

Snorre's brow was a gently curving arch that thrust
against his bushy, light brown eyebrows. His eyes lay deep
in his head, as if his gaze wished to hide itself away. His
eyelids were fleshy and red. He sat up with a start. What
was that noise? Carefully, he got out of bed. He dressed
quickly. Could it have been Margrete's horse, or Orækja's?
That would be too good to be true. Even half asleep, he
hadn't forgotten the sight of Sleipnir.

Why hadn't he heard from his old friend Sturla Bårdsson
recently? He could have done with him just now. Sturla had
always told him that whenever he was worried about Orækja
or burdened with other cares, he should comfort himself
with the thought that, deep down, he was a son of the soil
who'd made himself into what he was. His friend's well-
intentioned advice was useless.

He looked out, almost by chance. Who had lit all those
torches? He could make out Kyrre and Gyda. Who were
the others? Where had they been hiding recently? Weren't
there more of them? The carpenter, the shepherd and even
the sailmaker, employed in constantly repairing the ship
Duke Skúli had given him, were outside. They were
approaching the south gate. What were they up to? Kyrre
was even raising his hands in the air, as if to show he wasn't
bearing arms. They halted in the middle of the yard. He

couldn't hear what was being said. They were removing their footwear! He stooped, inching a little to the right to get a better view. What was the matter with them? They continued, barefoot, towards the gate, past the remains of Sleipnir and the clouded pool. But who was following them? They were carrying swords and had knives in their belts. Several had bows across their shoulders and quivers of arrows on their backs. Why hadn't anyone stopped them? Some were pointing in his direction. He ducked and crept over to the long bench. What were they thinking of?

Tumi, Sturla and Oraekja couldn't be far away. It wouldn't be long before these intruders got a surprise! At Saudafjell, Snorre and the three others had sealed a mutual defence pact. It was only a matter of patience. They'd come, all right. Naturally, they'd let them enter Reykholt, enticing them into a trap. The three of them would soon arrive with hundreds of men. He paced up and down by the table. He would just have to endure it, let the time pass and make himself scarce.

Of course they'd come! Who was leading the men outside? He went over to the hole in the wall, stood on tip-toe and peeped quickly out. There, at the back, someone was talking. The others were nodding. Was it possible! Could it really be him? Quickly, Snorre ducked again. He didn't want to see. He'd already seen. The man leading the force outside with the utmost resolve, it was him. Snorre's own guards were nowhere to be seen. Swine! Cowards! And there, just behind the leader, was it true? He'd never seen him bearing arms. But there was no room for doubt! Snorre was on the verge of tearing open the door and yelling at him. Torkild was talking to a man he'd never seen before. Only now did he understand! He was surrounded, his throat constricted, as if an encircling rope was being tightened.

Life doesn't end happily. But it's good that it does have an end. Snorre wasn't able to realize that he would actually gain by dying. For a long time he'd said that he wasn't afraid of death, but that he'd prefer not to be present.

Snorre's pacings next to the table got shorter and shorter. His breath was heavy and irregular. He must do it. Orækja must save him! If only he could manage it! He had to strike them down, brutally and mercilessly, without hesitation.

'Orækja,' he shouted. 'I'm depending on you, my son. Come! There's no time to lose. I haven't done anything to deserve your devotion, but come for God's sake,' and after a brief pause, 'Yes, you are my son.'

He stood motionless in the centre of the room. He was panting. In his mind's eye, Snorre saw a powerful white horse struggling in a bog. For a time, it struggled, trying to find firm ground under its hooves. The harder it tried, the deeper it sank until it disappeared.

The valley of Reykholt had always been visited by misfortune, ever since Torlaug had married Torir Torsteinsson almost a century earlier. Their children were healthy at birth, but after a while they died. Weighed down with sorrow, Torlaug made a pilgrimage to Rome. Her husband didn't particularly want to go, but because he loved his wife, he accompanied her. During the journey she gave birth to a child in Norway. They left the child in the care of some old acquaintances. But neither of its parents returned. First, Torir succumbed in Rome, and then Torlaug in Lucca, after praying to the Volto Santo crucifix. The day before, she'd learnt that her sole surviving child had died in Norway. Her father, the priest Táll Sölvason, believed he had a claim on his daughter's considerable fortune. Her husband's relatives maintained that they were the only ones with a right to anything. They used Snorre's father, Sturla, to advance their case. Arbitration at Reykholt was decided upon. After negotiating for an entire morning and afternoon, Táll's wife, Torgerdur, thought there'd been enough talk. The priest's wife got hold of a knife and stabbed Sturla. She wanted to make him look like the character he resembled most, namely Odin. That was what she screamed at any rate, as she aimed the knife at his eye. She missed. Before being overpowered, she had managed to inflict a nasty wound on Sturla's cheek. Táll, who'd already lost his daughter, his son-in-law and all his grandchildren, said that Sturla could name his own compensation for his wife's attack. Ordinarily, twenty-five or thirty head of cattle would have been the usual price for an unprovoked murder. Sturla demanded ten times as much. Táll protested that Sturla hadn't died in the attack. To no avail. The next step would have been civil war. But the Icelandic chieftains had little stomach for more fighting. The greatest of them, Jon Loptsson of Oddi, was asked to mediate in the affair, as both parties trusted him. He offered to bring up Sturla's three-year-old son, Snorre. His father accepted the offer.

Snorre had never been so frightened before. He didn't know where to turn for help. His people had surrendered and deserted Reykholt bare-footed, without resistance, they'd trotted through the gate like sheep, away from their master, past Sleipnir's remains, through the gate and out of sight. Jesus had only had one Judas. He had an entire flock of them. How many were there? Twenty? Six men on horseback were approaching. How many might there be in all? He began to sweat. His temples pounded.

Torkild smiled at the man standing next to him.

They whispered to one another. The dark-haired man could hear that, suddenly, Torkild had begun to speak of Snorre in the past tense.

The men outside were so confident of victory that they were talking and shouting. Snorre could hear practically every word. In the dimly lit room, he crossed to the table. He gripped its top with both hands. First he raised his right leg onto the bench, then his left. Standing precariously on the bench, he stared through the topmost peep-hole at the man leading the throng in the yard outside. There must be more than fifty of them! Even more were arriving! It must be closer to seventy. There was the leader again. There could be no doubt—it was Gissur Thorvaldsson. What was it he'd dreamt yesterday night? Hadn't Gissur figured in his dream? Wasn't Kolbeinn standing next to Gissur? He didn't realize that he would never get an answer. He reproached Gissur for his thirst for power and fancied he could catch the stench of his former sons-in-law, even from where he stood concealed. Gissur, a man he'd always embraced each time they'd met.

If only Tumi, Sturla and Orækja could get there! They had to manage it.

Snorre and Gissur had run into each other at Thingvellir a few months earlier. The atmosphere had been pleasant and relaxed. They had shaken hands, spoken with affection in their voices about Little Jon and repeated that in troubled times it was good that at least the two of them were friends. Gissur had done most of the talking. Several times, he emphasized the esteem in which he held Snorre. For one tiny moment, Snorre had asked himself if all these words mightn't be a cloak for something else. This thought evaporated as quickly as it had arrived. Snorre stood there lapping up the adulation. He liked it. True, he lowered his eyes when the praise seemed almost too lavish. But he refuted nothing. He'd let his eyelids hide his pleasure like an embarrassed boy.

Suddenly, Gissur had fallen silent. He'd looked as if he might be harbouring a secret. He seemed to be debating whether to share it with Snorre. Snorre wondered what he was thinking about. Hesitantly, Gissur asked him to convey his best wishes to Hallveig, who he'd heard was gravely ill. Snorre replied that it wasn't as bad as all that, but that he would pass the greetings on. His trip to the Althing had been in doubt for a long time. They began talking about the saddles they used and the relative merits of their saddlers. The words passed more and more half-heartedly between them. Now he understood why Gissur's expression had become so remote after a while!

Snorre was the one who took his leave first. He mounted Sleipnir. As he was the senior, it was only right and proper that he took the initiative. He clicked his tongue at Sleipnir and pulled on the reins. They smiled and waved briefly. That was the last they'd seen of each other.

Gissur had a secret. And he'd been on the point of divulging it. He'd kept it for almost a year and had wrestled with himself, this way and that, about whether to tell Snorre. For a while, he'd considered the possibility of taking some of his closest family into his confidence first. Maybe they could help him come to a decision. He might need support. Snorre would certainly have paid him handsomely to know what was in the air. No matter what he decided, it would have serious consequences. Did he really wish, in the depths of his soul, that he'd never had that letter from

King Håkon? Ever since he'd received it, he'd been wracked with doubt. He unrolled it several times and studied the neatly formed characters on the parchment. Gissur had been overwhelmed by the power vested in him. The letter was like a magic sword. After a few weeks he began to feel surprised that he'd been given the task. Then his suspicions grew. Was this an attempt to test him? Could it be a trap? It wasn't long before he was able to establish that the letter was genuine, and that it must be regarded as an order. If it wasn't obeyed, misfortune would be visited on him. Autumn, winter and spring passed and still he couldn't make up his mind. The meeting with Snorre at the Althing had decided him. Snorre's gentle eyes that afternoon, the fond memories they shared of Little Jon, and his own wedding at Reykholt so many years before, made things difficult for Gissur.

He asked Snorre if there hadn't been a wedding at the end of May, between Hallveig's sister and the youngest Sighvatr boy. Gissur knew there had been, but he had to find something to say.

Snorre made no reply but explained that he must press on, as he'd promised to meet the lawspeaker. There was no time for anything more than a farewell. Snorre had become easy meat during the past year. There were few lurking dangers. He'd aged visibly, he looked like a walrus with heavy eyelids. And Orækja had become dangerous and unpredictable. It was even more obvious now that Snorre could no longer control his son. Snorre's power and influence seemed to be crumbling. His brothers and his family weren't as strongly united as they had been and, finally, at Reykholt, as at the farms surrounding it, many of the workers had run away or begun to oppose him without his knowledge. When Snorre didn't have Oraekja near at hand, he was vulnerable.

Immediately after Gissur thought he'd made his decision, the doubts had come. Would he be able to gather enough men? Were there sufficient capable men who hated Snorre enough to want to kill him? When he began recruiting people, he'd have to stress that Oraekja's crimes had been directed by Snorre. All the time he'd been looking into Snorre's eyes, he couldn't contemplate the notion of killing him. But watching the heavy, sluggish, ageing form from behind, he was reminded of how easy it would be, and how short the road was to becoming Iceland's most powerful man. Once Gissur had seen the broad back and Sleipnir's whisking tail, the old man's fate was sealed.

King Håkon had sent the letter a couple of weeks after the fall of Duke Skúli. The man who arrived with the royal letter was another of Snorre's sons-in-law—one he'd had less to do with than Gissur or Kolbeinn. Like Kolbeinn, he'd been married to Hallbera. Hallbera had divorced Arni the Fickle'. Arni couldn't forgive either Hallbera or her father for this. Arni felt spurned. He needed the position that the marriage had given him. That autumn, Arni had told several people that Snorre was greedy enough to sell his daughter twice over. Now, the former son-in-law wanted revenge.

Snorre had found Kolbeinn easier to deal with. It wasn't Kolbeinn's fault that Hallbera became terminally ill. Snorre had almost felt pity for him. When the letter was delivered, Gissur looked to see if Arni had broken the king's seal. He was capable of it, he thought, but fortunately the seal was undamaged.

Five years earlier, Gissur had killed the king's own bailiff in Iceland, Sturla Sighvatsson. In 1233, after the king had lost all hope of Snorre keeping his promise to incorporate Iceland under the Norwegian crown, he had given the role to Snorre's nephew, Sturla. In Håkon's eyes, Gissur was probably the best candidate, precisely because he'd had the courage to defy the king's command. It was a case of winning him over to his side and holding out the opportunity of becoming the top man in Iceland. That Gissur and his clan of Haukdøls had, according to several envoys, developed an abiding hatred of the Sturlungs was an added recommendation. The king didn't hesitate long. Sturla Sighvatsson's killer was the right person to enforce the royal will.

Over the next two days, Gissur came close to changing his mind, but from the third day, once he saw how easy it was to attract supporters, he was implacable.

Almost a generation had passed since Snorre had given his promise to Skúli and Håkon, but it was only six years before that the king had got Skúli to recognize that Snorre would never carry out the task. The king's letter told Gissur to try to bring Snorre back to Norway alive. If this proved impossible, he was to be killed. King Håkon wrote that from now on Snorre was to be considered a 'landrádamadr', a traitor.

Snorre's two sons-in-law, Gissur and Kolbeinn, had met a few days earlier on the backbone of mountains that divided the country between east and west. There, they'd laid the final plan. Gissur quickly collected the men he needed. Ormr and Klængr, Gissur's two nephews, Loftr, the bishop's son who'd elected to throw in his lot with the poor and Arni the Fickle were amongst the willing assasins. With the whole force gathered around him, some miles north-west of Reykholt, he mounted a great slab of rock. Raising his voice, he read out the letter from the Norwegian king. When Gissur announced that he'd been appointed the king's 'skutilsvein', his jarl in Iceland, the men standing closest began nodding first, before the nods were taken up by the others. He asked if anyone thought it possible to transport Snorre voluntarily to Norway. They all shook their heads, apart from Ormr. Gissur wasn't certain how to interpret this. He took a couple of steps towards Ormr and whispered: 'Is there something you want to say to me alone?'

Now Ormr did shake his head. 'It's nothing, just some work on the farm I need to do.'

Klængr stood guarantor that Ormr wouldn't inform on them. A few minutes later, Gissur told him in a whisper that he could go. If there was too much fuss about Ormr's volte-face, it might encourage further doubters in the flock. That must be avoided at all costs. Gissur feared they might be assailed by the same ambivalence that he'd struggled with for more than a year.

Klængr tugged at Gissur's jerkin and asked if it might be possible to have a look at the king's seal. Gissur wondered what the problem was. Had Klængr got cold feet, as well? Hesitantly, Gissur unrolled the parchment with the king's seal at the bottom. Klængr ran his fingers over the handwriting and down to the reddish-brown seal. The small bulge showed the figure of a young king, seated on a throne. In his right hand he held a sword pointing straight up. A Latin text around the image announced it to be Håkon IV Håkonsson, king of Norway.

Gissur was losing patience. Klængr again ran his fingers over the seal and then studied the illustration of the Norwegian king and the text around it. Ormr, who'd been about to get on his horse, was taken aback when Klængr spent so long with Gissur. He walked back and saw Gissur's perplexed expression. Ormr stationed himself behind his brother. Gissur asked quietly: 'Are you backing out too, Klængr?'

'Not at all, it's just that I've never seen a royal seal before.'

Gissur sent two brothers to Borgarfjord to reconnoitre. One was Arni the Scornful and the other Svartr. Some months earlier, Svartr had been tricked by Orækja in a deal over cattle. The brothers had ridden to his father at Reykholt to recover the money. Snorre had summoned his son, who happened to be staying the night at the estate. Orækja drew his sword. Arni received a long gash across his upper back before the brothers got away.

Not far from Borg, where in his time Snorre had married Herdis, the daughter of a wealthy priest called Bersi, Arni and Svartr spied a man with a slight stoop in the distance. He had tied his horse to a sturdy bush. They thought they recognized him. They moved behind a knoll, scrambled down from their horses and whispered to each other. Could he really be alone? It was impossible. He was usually sur-rounded by able-bodied minders. He seemed to be pacing about talking to himself. His mouth opened occasionally. He was shaking his head, waving his arms and mumbling. It almost looked as if he was swearing. He raised his eyes to the sky and stamped.

They couldn't hear him. His horse whinnied. It had realized there were others in the vicinity. The two brothers stroked their horses' muzzles to calm them and prevent them answering. Neither of them was carrying a bow and arrows. They each had a sword, knives and a spear fixed to the saddle. As fighting men, they were by no means inexperienced. But the man a couple of hundred yards away, although deep in thought, carried a bow and was one of Iceland's deadliest and most practised warriors.

Arni and Svartr had been sent out as scouts because they were skilled riders. They rode fast and tirelessly, and knew how to use their horses to their best advantage. They had, above all, to avoid any clashes. If they gave away what was planned at Reykholt, they would pay with their lives. They needed to get a closer look at the man. If it was Oraekja, they'd have to ride back to Gissur as fast as they could.

Gissur wanted Oraekja as far away as possible when he struck. If Oraekja managed to give them the slip, they could assume that he and his men would ambush Gissur. The brothers agreed that Svartr would have to crawl closer to make certain it was Oraekja. Arni would hold the horses ready. If Svartr was taken prisoner, Arni was to ride at top speed to warn Gissur, without trying to save his brother. If this happened, the order was clear. Svartr would have to take his own life. Svartr moved gingerly round the knoll and crawled forward. His gaze alternating between the horse and the man who was talking to himself. When he wasn't speaking loudly and angrily, there were long periods when he just stood still, and then they'd hear a sniff. Was he weeping?

Oraekja moved between two large bushes stretching out a net. What was he doing? Svartr looked at his horse. It made no sound but it pawed the ground uneasily. He noticed two baskets on the horse's rump. He was setting a bird-trap! Svartr looked at the man again. Yes, it was Oraekja all right. He trembled. Oraekja snapped a twig. Oraekja gazed

in his direction. If Orækja saw him, he could easily get him
with an arrow. There was no doubting that Orækja was one
of Iceland's best bowmen. From a young boy, he'd boasted
that one day he'd be as good a shot as Egil Skallagrimsson,
the daring hero of *Egil's Saga*.

Orækja turned to face directly towards him. Svartr
held his breath. Had he seen him? Orækja stood stock still.
Svartr lay on his stomach. He felt the moss aginst his chin.
His eyes staring through small branches of heather. He
saw greens and browns. There in front of him stood Orækja,
constantly stroking the bridge of his nose with his forefinger
and clearing his throat. Snorre's own mad son. The unpredictable warrior, his father's thoroughly loyal tool, out
hawking alone. Orækja had set up the trap, a net stretched
between the bushes about six feet from the ground and
right in front of him. Svartr forced his face down into the
heather. He could hear the two grouse that served as decoys
in the net. Svartr was wearing a grey cap. He hoped that
the cap and the brown breeches and jacket would make
him blend into the landscape. The sounds the grouse were
making gave Svartr the courage to breathe again. He smelt
the dry earth. The heather tickled and pricked his nose
and cheeks. Now he could make out the sound of Orækja
mumbling. He came closer. The footsteps stopped. Svartr
heard a flapping overhead. The footsteps receeded. He
peeped quickly across the heather.

A grey hunting falcon circled the two grouse in the
snare. The falcon hovered, lost a little height and shot out
its head and bill before stooping, its wings pressed tight
against its body. Svartr saw grouse feathers flying and caught
a glimpse of the falcon's wing in the net. Orækja ran up. He
was wearing a glove on his right hand. He loosened the
rope which held the net. He grasped the greedy falcon in

his right hand. Before the grouse had been half eaten he'd succeeded in pulling off the hacking bird. Svartr could see that Orækja was trying to get the falcon into one of the baskets on the horse. But before Orækja managed to close the lid of the basket, the falcon got loose and flew off.

It was then that Svartr should have taken to his heels. Instead, he remained where he was. Orækja turned and walked towards him. He pushed his face into the heather and held his breath. He could hear the vegetation just in front of him being pressed down. If he lifted his head to check how close Orækja was, he would be risking dreadful torture and divulging everything he knew. If he were found lying on his stomach with his head in the undergrowth, it would be impossible to find any excuse. Orækja would immediately realize that he was there to spy on him, and that he would be reporting to someone. Orækja wouldn't give up before he'd got the name of his taskmaster.

Although Orækja hadn't seen anything disturbing the last time he'd been at Reykholt, he was extremely suspicious. And he was certain that he and his father would be friends again. Because his father was wise, everything would come right in the end.

Svartr forced his eyes tight shut. He could hear Orækja's heavy breath. Orækja stopped. Silence fell. Svartr tried to swallow, then changed his mind. If he swallowed, it would be heard for miles around. His mouth went dry. There was a thumping in his head. He had no idea where the thumping came from. His brother, the horses, they all must be able to hear how his blood, heart, joints, bones, everything was thumping inside him. His eyes and heart were being pressed down into the heather and the earth, all the way down to the fiery hell beneath. Orækja stood still.

Had he been discovered? Perhaps he should play dead. Or jump up and run as hard as he could to the horse. Arni had already untied it and was holding it by the reins. Should he play dead or run? He opened his eyes warily. He'd pushed his sword beneath his body when he'd begun crawling. It was pressing into his chest and thigh. Orækja walked towards the vague patch of grey and brown in the heather. He was mumbling about going home to his father, and if he wasn't let in, at least keeping the estate under observation. It had been oddly silent the last time he'd been there. He yawned.

Had somebody thrown away some clothing? He went closer. It looked like a man. A corpse out here on the moors? His eyes searched around him. A grouse took to the wing. Otherwise, there wasn't a soul to be seen. Was this why the horse had been anxious? It could even sense dead men. He glanced over at his horse, blinked an eye and raised his right leg over the grey cap. He placed his foot on Svartr's back. It was certainly a cadaver. A dead human body. He'd never stood on a dead man. Presumably there wasn't much difference between one that was dead and one that was alive? He pressed his right foot into the back of the prostrate body. It wasn't a firm foothold. He pushed his foot down even harder. He'd been a lean man. Did he know him? He crouched. He rolled Svartr onto his side. He couldn't have been dead long. The colour in his face was almost normal. He was a little pale, but it couldn't have been more than a day. He didn't seem to have injuries from swords or arrows. His clothes seemed intact. He wasn't very old. He'd dropped dead in the prime of life. His sword hadn't been used. He didn't recognize him. Or did he? It was easy to forget that people could die peacefully too, that life could simply ebb away, without any explanation, and the riddle remain unsolved within the dead body. Many in Iceland wished for such a peaceful death. His own father had spoken of it several times. The man in front of him might have drawn his last breath early today. Perhaps yesterday evening. No earlier. He rose.

Orækja's horse reared up on its hind legs, whinnied and tossed back its head. Orækja turned, soothed the horse and told it to calm down. Svartr opened his eyelids a crack. Orækja was standing a couple of yards away. He was looking at the horse. Svartr was convinced that his final moment had come. From some unknown place in the clouds above, fate intervened. A falcon hove into view. The horse tugged. Orækja walked rapidly across the heather. He'd have to come back later and look at the face. Orækja tried to grab the reins. The horse danced around him in a circle.

Svartr jumped to his feet and ran for the bush. Orækja swung the bow from his shoulder. With lightning speed, one hand reached for an arrow from the quiver. He set the arrow against the string. The other hand gripped the bow tightly. Orækja drew the bow and aimed. He sighted the man's back as he leapt over heather and undergrowth. He aimed at the top left corner. Orækja shouted. Svartr kept on running. Orækja aimed and shot. The arrow went wide. Svartr ran into the bushes. Orækja swore and took out another arrow. He heard the neigh of a horse. It couldn't be his own. Where was the sound coming from? There, behind the mound, the man had hidden a horse. At a wild gallop, he took off in a westerly direction. And there was another horse and rider! He aimed and hit the foremost rider in the right shoulder. The rider gave a scream and fell forward on to his horse's neck, but didn't come off. Orækja reached for another arrow, aimed at the second rider, shot and missed.

By the time Orækja finally managed to calm his horse, the riders were out of sight. Were they bondsmen who'd been trying to rob him? They had ridden in the opposite direction to Reykholt. They probably didn't know who he was. In all likelihood, he wouldn't recognize the other rider, either. He followed them a little way to see whether the injured man had fallen off. After scaling the first hilltop he gave up, rode calmly back and set another trap.

Snorre glimpsed two men riding hard through the gate of Reykholt. One of them was clinging to his horse's neck. As soon as the horse came to a halt, he fell off and lay still. He was bleeding from the shoulder. The other rider dismounted with great difficulty. He remained for a long time with his legs straight and his body bent forward. It looked as if he were trying to catch his breath. Gissur questioned him about something. Snorre tried to make out if he knew the pair. They were too far away. Maybe he'd met them at one time. Many people had wanted to shake his hand, but he couldn't recall their faces. The man who'd been bending now straightened, said something to Gissur and pointed. Was that Orækja's name Snorre had caught? He fixed his attention on Gissur, he'd relaxed his shoulders. He seemed relieved. Snorre went down on his hands and knees, lowered his torso and put his ear against the crack at the bottom of the door. Might he be able to hear better like this? He tried to position his right ear as close as possible to the chink between the bottom of the door and the doorstep.

He was able to catch a few words. Gissur was speaking. Someone had asked why they didn't strike immediately. Gissur replied that he didn't know how many men Snorre had guarding him in the main house. None, someone shouted. Snorre wasn't certain if it was Kyrre's voice. He clutched at his chest. He breathed a little more easily after telling himself that help would surely be at hand. Gissur said that Snorre probably had men who would defend him to the last drop of their blood. There were protests. Yes, that was Kyrre all right. Gissur still didn't believe him. Snorre tried to see if he could recognize Orækja's voice outside. All things considered, he was glad that he couldn't hear him. How could he harbour such thoughts about Orækja! His son must be close by, with an even larger force than Gissur's.

What he needed was a flying army of hunting falcons. An army of the very best sort, white hunting falcons from Greenland. Hunting falcons which obeyed his orders alone. Falcons which, at a given signal, would take to the sky over Reykholt. Two hundred would have been sufficient. Not a few lonely sparrows, not a few wise owls, nor yet audacious ravens or crows and certainly not peaceful doves. No, they must be hunting falcons with all their speed, strength and piercing gaze. They could be positioned on the roof under an enormous blanket. The torches would reflect light on the faces and eyes of Gissur's men and horses. As soon as the covering was pulled away the falcons would spot them. There was no better weapon than a hunting falcon. With lethal force, they'd find their mark with purpose and pre-cision. First, the falcons would mount high into the air and circle the yard before stooping. Half of them would settle on the horses' hindquarters, hacking until they reached the liver, whereupon the horses would drop dead. The other birds would pluck out the eyes of Gissur's men. He'd read of the Byzantine emperor who'd ordered that all his defeated Bulgarian enemies should be blinded, apart from one who would conduct them back to Sofia. That was the way to do it. He would blind each of Gissur's men, apart from one, so that he could lead them away from Reykholt. Everything would have been settled in a few minutes. If you owned a hunting falcon you were never alone. If you owned several, you were a rich man. Snorre had none. As he crouched with his ear against the crack under the door, barely even an insect was near at hand.

Suddenly a voice came out of the darkness immediately behind him. It was a long time since he'd heard it last. It was the voice that had advised him against travelling back to Iceland two years ago. Now it was telling him that his time had finally come. He still hadn't learnt to understand himself, much less his son or the people around him. But he'd pretended to understand an entire people, and to write about them even though they lived across the sea. What arrogance! Without asking himself a single question, he'd described in detail their kings' motives and attitudes over several centuries. He had, without a moment's hesitation, taken it upon himself to enlighten the lives of everyone on 'the disc of the earth' with his own wisdom. He should know that he hadn't managed to set spark to a single word.

Was it King Håkon speaking? No, the voice was older, much older.

Snorre was asked if now, just as he was about to draw his final breath, he'd become wise enough to see that he could have profited from the humility of the sheep. It is neither vain, conceited nor greedy.

He was about to turn and reply. The voice had gone.

Snorre got up off his hands and knees. He breathed heavily and managed to scramble upright.

He waited until all was dark outside. They'd obviously concluded that he was in the feasting hall of the main house. The previous evening, it had begun to cloud over.

The night wouldn't be bright or starry. He took with him the lantern that stood by the long hearth. The lamp gave only a feeble light. Black night would save him. It would give the greedy dogs out there something to think about! He stroked his beard. They'd get a surprise. When they stormed in, he'd have vanished without a trace. The corners of his mouth lifted. A scornful chuckle filled the room. Outside it was pitch dark.

Snorre had been right—it was impossible to see a single star. A large carpet lay on the floor. The carpet had been woven by Hallveig and one of the servant girls. He could feel it with his foot. Snorre imagined its colours, red and grey. He'd always liked it. The motif was two capital S's with a dragon's head at each end of the letters. He dragged the carpet aside. He felt his way to the recessed handle of the trapdoor which had been covered by the carpet. He opened the trapdoor and stepped warily onto the first step. The stairs led down to the secret tunnel beneath the houses of Reykholt, and to Snorre's Bath. He felt his way in the dark. It was hard on his swollen feet. Briefly, he hovered on the top step, considering the advantages and drawbacks of taking the sword that hung on the wall. Should he go and get it? But if it came to a fight, what could he really do? He decided not to bother with the sword. They'd never find him! For several years he'd been building the tunnel system under Reykholt without the workers on the estate knowing anything about it. The only underground passage that was general knowledge was the one from the main house to the pool. Neither Kyrre nor Torkild had any inkling of the other secret tunnels. Had the priest given anything away? He didn't think so. He'd hired Norwegians to dig out the tunnel. They'd been sent home as soon as the work was finished.

He hadn't even told Margrete about them. He closed the trapdoor above him. Snorre descended a couple of steps and pulled at two rope-ends that were attached to the woven carpet which was now ingeniously drawn back into place above him. He took the lower two steps and went down a long subterranean passage. He could walk practically upright the whole way. After a while, the passage rose slightly, until it came to a stone stair. At the top of this, he stood listening for a few moments before tugging at a rope. A door opened. The back of a small stack of firewood came into view. He removed the logs carefully, stepped through the doorway, shut the door and restacked the wood in front of it. Now, moving as silently as he could, he climbed to the first storey and pushed against a wall. The wall turned out to be a door, which gave on to a bedroom he called his 'Sleeping Den'. He lay down and listened. When would relief come? He fell asleep, completely exhausted.

Before the first glimmerings of day, Gissur's men broke into the main house. The men were enraged when they found Snorre wasn't there. They ran amok, smashing the ornaments on the tables. They hurled the books to the floor, upset the long table, threw candlesticks on the hearth and ripped up every bit of clothing they could find, but it didn't do anything to help. Snorre had disappeared. With roars and yells and stamping of feet they stormed about, shouting that they knew where he was. With torches and lights they searched for the hiding place of Snorre's bodyguards.

Gissur kept his worries to himself. He felt a growing sense of unease. Had he misjudged the situation? Had Snorre managed to escape with his bodyguards after all? Who'd said he'd seen Snorre inside the main house in the afternoon? He told Kolbeinn to find the young fellow immediately. Kyrre was brought to him. Gissur studied him narrowly. He didn't recognize him. He looked to be in his mid-twenties. Old enough to be a seasoned traitor. Gissur tried to speak calmly. The hair of the man facing him was plastered to his head with sweat. Kyrre said nothing. He tried to listen. He had to catch every word. Kyrre could tell from Gissur's eyes that his life hung in the balance. His heart was pounding so hard that he kept losing more and more of the words. Each time he was asked about something, he nodded or said yes. It wasn't always the right answer. Kyrre saw how Gissur Thorvaldsson's head was beginning to quiver. It was getting redder. The colour of his face emphasized the whites of his eyes.

Who had vouchsafed that this young man knew where Snorre was the whole time? A call went out for Torkild. Gissur knew him at any rate. He'd offered the skilled smith work in the forge on his own estate. Gissur's face had almost returned to its normal colour. Torkild said that he knew nothing but good of Kyrre, young he might be, but he could be trusted.

Torkild's well-intentioned words increased Gissur's suspicions. Why didn't Kyrre know where Snorre was if he was working on the estate? He told Torkild to leave. Gissur beckoned to one of the men standing closest to him. He whispered in the white-haired man's ear. The man went off to the quarters where most of the food at Reykholt was prepared. Gissur continued to face Kyrre. Gissur didn't look at him. He looked past him. Occasionally he would send a glance after the white-haired man. Kyrre's mouth got drier. He didn't dare blink, for fear of what might happen in the instant he wasn't looking straight ahead. The white-haired man returned. Kyrre fainted. He crumpled like an empty sack. Torkild tried to force his way over to

Gissur. A couple of sturdy men pushed him back. The white-haired man was carrying a sword. Its tip was red hot.

Svartr and Arni approached and raised him up. Svartr could only support him with one arm. His shoulder had been treated and bandaged. The injury in no way diminished his eagerness to serve. Svartr asked if they should remove his clothing. Gissur didn't answer. Svartr wanted to know if they should at least roll up his sleeves. Gissur shook his head. There was no problem, the sword would go through the clothing. He laughed. Svartr sent his brother a doubtful look.

Torkild shouted that even if Kyrre hadn't known as much as he thought, he was the only one who was thoroughly acquainted with every nook and cranny of Reykholt. Weren't they intending to go from house to house?

'What about you?' Gissur asked. Torkild opened his arms wide and said that he only knew the forge and the house that he and his wife lived in. He'd never been around Snorre and his circle. Over the past few months, Kyrre had had much more to do with him. Also, it was Kyrre who had broken Sleipnir in and taken care of him. Kyrre had had a good excuse for entering the main building unannounced to discuss the horses and the daily tasks, amongst other things.

Kyrre sank to his knees. He shut his eyes so as to avoid looking at the glowing sword tip. Terror choked off the imploring words he so much wanted to fend off the looming agony.

A messenger rode up. His horse halted in front of Gissur. The messenger related that Orækja had ridden to Borg and had gone to bed for the night. The message placated Gissur a little. But as soon as Torkild suggested that

Kyrre should begin to go through the houses, he got angry. He grabbed the sword out of the white-haired man's hand and laid it against Kyrre's right shoulder. The sword burnt through the clothing and skin. The smell of burnt wool and flesh mingled with Kyrre's screams. Gissur lifted the sword from the young shoulder and turned to Torkild.

'Who makes the decisions here?'

'Wise man that you are, Gissur, you surely want your underlings to speak their minds?' And Torkild added after a pause: 'When it's to your own advantage.'

Gissur made no reply.

Torkild took this to signify agreement, and began to move in Kyrre's direction to tend him. He'd only got a couple of yards before he suddenly screamed like a banshee. Gissur had thrown the knife he carried in his belt, straight through his right foot. Blood was welling up through the lace-holes. Gissur asked if it was Torkild or him who gave the order to move? Torkild sat down on the ground, clutching his foot in both hands. The blood ran over his ankle and made the surrounding grass sticky.

'You threw it!' Torkild shouted.

'Give me back the knife,' said Gissur.

Torkild was tossing his head from side to side. His face was white. Svartr bent and quickly pulled the knife out and handed it to Gissur. Gissur stood over the wailing Torkild. He looked at Torkild, shook his head and then drew the white-haired man a little to one side. He wanted to hear what the older man had to say. Gissur beckoned Kyrre to him. The older man called for the two who'd dressed Svartr's wound. Kyrre was told to take off his upper garments. The pain was too great for him to pull the blue tunic over his head. Arni helped him remove the garment.

Getting it over his head was easier than separating the material from the wound underneath. They ripped it off. Kyrre yelled. Instead of trying to remove the wool from the burn, the men covered the wound with a herbal salve. They also had a jar of aloe vera extract which they carefully applied to the part of the burn that was open. A linen dressing was placed over the wound and the bits of material. Gissur had realized that he needed Kyrre in the continuing hunt for Snorre.

Kyrre's piercing cries had woken Snorre. It took him a few seconds to work out where he was. He sat up in bed. He was a terrified refugee in Reykholt! Carefully, he climbed off the bed. Through the peephole he could see some of the men below. They were pointing. Wasn't one of them pointing right at him? Did one of them know about the door behind the wood stack? He'd lain down with his clothes on. He had to reach the underground passage. He couldn't stay here. He sat on the bed and did up his boot laces. How short of breath he was! He held on to the bedpost with one hand and heaved himself to his feet. Again, he peered through the hole in the wall. A man was still pointing in his direction.

He had to leave quickly. He crept out the same way he'd come. From the stairs he could see that they'd lit torches. Snorre didn't want to light his lantern before he was down in the passage. He fumbled in the darkness to find the concealing wall and descended all the stone steps. There were three alternatives and three houses to choose from. He decided to travel underground to the westernmost house. It was rarely used. As soon as he'd lit the candle in the lamp, he made the decision.

Could he remember the knack of getting in? With his own hands he had made this wooden panelling with its special secret. Torkild had forged one of the locks following Snorre's directions, but without knowing what it was to be used for. A smile of triumph spread across Snorre's face at the recollection. Then his eyes became focused again, and he concentrated the last of his strength in getting himself inside his new hiding place. He ascended the winding stairs. He stood in front of the door which could only be opened if pressure was applied to the upper left-hand corner.

Snorre couldn't remember which of the corners he was supposed to press. He put his lamp down, and fumbled for a long time, pushing carefully several times. Without success. He shoved harder and listened. No reaction. He stood there, now feeling the top left-hand corner with the flat of his hand, before pushing again. The door opened. It was dark in the room. He stood fearfully just inside the doorway. He couldn't remember if a light could be seen from outside. He took a few hesitant steps before recalling the room. Fortunately. There were so many rooms to keep track of, but he was certain. Light couldn't be seen from outside this room. The tongue of flame burnt silently, licking at the air in the room. The beam of light revealed most of it.

There was someone there! He turned. A man was sitting on the floor in the corner. He'd covered his head with his hands. A half-eaten loaf of bread was in front of him and a large, green bottle lay on its side. The man sat leaning forward as if waiting for the *coup de grâce*. At first Snorre couldn't see who it was. The man hardly raised his head. He had no weapon.

'Is it you?' Snorre said in a low voice.

The priest lowered his hands.

'So this is where you've been for the past few days, is it?' Snorre asked.

'You must whisper,' said Arnbjørn.

'I was looking forward to your sermon on the blessed martyr, Saint Maurice. I was especially interested to see if you were once more going to emphasize how strong his faith was when the lions tore him to pieces beneath the Roman emperor's tribune.' Snorre drew breath, his eyes were full of tears.

'I wanted to hear you tell it this year as well, Arnbjørn, even though I've heard it many times before.'

In the light from the lamp it was easy to see that Arnbjørn's face was white. The priest couldn't look him in the eyes. Between them lay a question that hadn't yet been broached. As soon as it left Snorre's lips, the contact between them would be severed for ever. If Arnbjørn wanted, he could have provided an explanation to which Snorre could have reconciled himself. As the situation stood, he would have accepted almost any story.

'Did you know that Gissur and his men were on their way?' Snorre asked.

There was a crash. A door below had been forced open. They could hear tables and chairs being upended. Suddenly Snorre became completely calm, as if all the life had run out of his body. What should he do?

'Hide in the secret passage you came by,' Arnbjørn said.

So he could still speak! Snorre was about to ask if he'd mentioned the tunnel to anyone else. Several crashes from below caused him to hurry out, down the concealed staircase behind the wall and into the long passage.

Not long after, Gissur and his men found Arnbjørn. Gissur
stood before the priest and asked where Snorre was.
Arnbjørn was still pale. In a gentle voice, Gissur asked
again if he knew of Snorre's whereabouts. Arnbjørn shook
his head cautiously. His crucifix hung from a chain round
his neck. It was made of silver decorated with rock-crystal
pearls. Arnbjørn the priest fingered the crucifix carefully.
Gissur asked why he'd hidden. He replied that he always
tried to keep away from conflict. All he wanted was silence
and peace, and a church to preach in. Nothing more. As
soon as he'd realized that swords would be drawn at
Reykholt, he did what he'd always done, retreated or gone
to ground. That was just his nature. He regretted much
else besides. Gissur shrugged his shoulders and looked at
the men around him. He asked if anybody could verify
that this really was the priest of Reykholt. None of them
could. One of the men raised his spear. Gissur waved him
away and told them to fetch Kyrre. Once again, Gissur
asked in a level voice if the priest was aware of Snorre's
movements. For the second time Arnbjørn shook his head.
Gissur asked him to answer in plain words.

'No,' said the priest.

'I don't believe you!' Gissur roared.

He bent down, held the flaming torch in front of the
priest's eyes and shouted again. Kyrre appeared in the doorway. Gissur pointed at Arnbjørn and glanced at Kyrre. The
was no doubt about it. Kyrre nodded.

Outside, more men came riding into the yard. The
moon was pared to its rind up in the dark vault of the sky.
Gissur received the shouted message that Klængr Bjørnsson
had finally arrived with reinforcements from Kjalarnes.
Gissur asked Arnbjørn if he didn't think he'd better tell

him where Snorre was pretty soon. Gissur told the white-haired, sinewy man to heat up the sword. The priest got his tongue back. If he could leave and preach somewhere away from Reykholt, he might possibly remember where Snorre was.

Gissur looked at his men. They said nothing. Gissur announced loudly that he could do whatever he liked, provided he told them where Snorre was. But the sooner the better. Arnbjørn said that Snorre was behind the hidden door. He pointed. If they descended the stairs, they'd find a secret passage, and somewhere in there they'd find him. He also said that immediately they reached the tunnel, there was an incline that was surprisingly steep if one wasn't expecting it. After a bit it levelled out. Gissur asked how wide it was, how high, where it led to, and whether Snorre was alone. The priest answered everything he was asked.

Gissur sent five men down into the secret passage. They were Markus Mardarson, Simon the Riddle, Torsteinn Gudinason, Torainn Asgrimsson and the man he appointed leader—Arni the Scornful. Arni wanted his brother Svartr, too. Gissur refused the request. Svartr wasn't strong enough after the injury to his shoulder. With lit torches, they ran down the steps and along the passage. Torsteinn stumbled on the steep section. He got up quickly and ran after the others. It wasn't long before they found Snorre.

At first they were afraid. Snorre was gazing steadily at them. He was unarmed. Was it a trap after all? There must be men behind him. They came to a halt. They looked at one another. After a pause, Arni advanced towards Snorre. Arni looked around.

'So you're the ones who're going to do it,' Snorre said.

His voice was resigned but calm, as if he'd got the answer to a question he'd been pondering for the past twenty-four hours. Snorre didn't even raise his arms to protect himself. No one rushed forward to defend him. No armed men, no soldiers, no angels rushed in. Arni raised his sword. The others shouted encouragement to him, or berated Snorre.

People display the greatest talent and imagination when describing their enemies. What power is unleashed when the back is turned to the light and the mind occupied with its darkest thoughts.

Snorre considered that God should prove his existence, if he hadn't already done so, by striking him with a bolt of lightning before these miserable creatures could finish him off. But God had other matters to attend to. Death forced fear into his eyes and followed up in his mouth, a bitter bile that he had to swallow whether he wanted to or not. He couldn't reconcile or resign himself to the fact that they were going to kill him. He was only human. Wasn't he? His eyes took on a lifeless cast. He stared at the ground right under his feet. He'd been on this earth for more than sixty years.

'Strike hard!' Simon shouted.

'No striking,' said Snorre.

Arni dealt him the fatal blow. The wound showed from beneath the left ear to the hollow of the throat. Snorre looked at Arni, and then doubled up and sat on the ground with an expression of disbelief on his face. It was full of wonder that this was what death felt like, as it forced its way into his belly, usurping more and more space within him. He tried to raise his right arm. He couldn't. He bent forwards again. He did nothing more. His look became sadder, as if he felt ill. Then Torsteinn struck. Snorre made no further movements to avoid the next thrusts. Apart from a strange sneer which spread across his face. It seemed as if he were laughing at them as he bared his teeth, dark with blood. He tried to say something. His mouth produced nothing but blood and a few gurgling noises. He pictured Margrete and himself out riding on a warm summer's day. There was no wind. They were on their way to Bessastadir. He patted Sleipnir.

'You only ever want to ride that little horse,' Margrete said.

A couple of tremors ran through him before he became still, and closed his eyes.

All five of them drove at him in turn. Five deep wounds. His head had slumped to the side. He sat on the cold floor with his head at an angle and his back propped against the wall. They left him there and went up to Gissur. They didn't run. Gissur asked what Snorre's last words had been. They told him. He shrugged his shoulders and said nothing.

Torkild was standing directly behind Gissur. No sooner had he heard Arni's words than he ran to find Snorre. When he saw the skald's closed eyes, he smiled with relief.

Once Gissur the Haukdøl had executed the most famous of the Sturlungs, he hoped to be able to rule the country in peace. It wasn't to be. With the support of King Håkon and the help of Cardinal William of Sabina, the Sturlung Tordur 'the Garrulous' Sighvatsson became Iceland's most powerful man. He would, it was claimed, finally bring Iceland under the Norwegian crown. Nothing happened. King Håkon elevated Gissur to jarl in 1258. Gissur promised to bring Iceland under Norwegian rule, and pay taxes to the king. The peasants of Iceland would pay the taxes. Even though the Norwegian king was supposed to maintain Iceland's peace, protect the Icelandic legal code and send ships with supplies of goods and men when needed, it was still taxes to Norway that was the most concrete element of the agreement. Gissur imagined he'd be allowed to run an independent jarldom allied to Norway with himself as ruler. Simpleton. King Håkon gave Gissur a title and a sword to wave about, but nothing else. Gissur Thorvaldsson entered a monastery to find spiritual peace. He found nothing. It wasn't until 1262 that the Althing acknowledged King Håkon as Iceland's first king.

For the first few days, Orækja wailed or moaned or sat still and wept. His wife tried to console him by saying that his father had never cared about him. All he'd used him for was to carry out the murders he didn't dare commit himself. She attempted to persuade Orækja not to travel to Reykholt. 'They're waiting for you,' Arnbjørg said. She was right. He knew she was.

'I want to see Father one last time. I want to embrace him before it's too late,' he shouted.

She managed to keep him away from Reykholt until Christmas. But then Orækja rode off with about thirty men and burnt down the manor and killed Klængr, who'd taken over Reykholt. What he couldn't burn, he began destroying, until he was overpowered and taken prisoner. Orækja was disinherited and banished to Norway for a second time. Four years later, he died not far from Bjørgvin, peacefully—his heart simply stopped beating, not far from the spot where Little Jon had been fatally wounded.

Margrete had arrived back at the farm two days before. She'd been distraught, covering her face with her hands and saying they mustn't kill Snorre. Each time her husband tried to tell her there wasn't anyone there, and certainly no one who was going to kill Snorre, she pushed him away.

She'd seen them coming, she screamed. This went on the whole day. She wailed and moaned as if she'd been stabbed. She was distracted. He left the house. He heard her crying Snorre's name over and over again. In his fury he went some distance from the farm buildings to tether some horses. When he returned all was quiet. After a while he became uneasy and rushed indoors.

She wasn't there! The children were missing as well. He shouted for her, without getting any reply. In a frenzy of fear, he tore round the farm to see where they were. Anything to put off looking over the cliff half a mile west of the farm. He walked faster and faster until he was running. Breathless, he peered over the precipice. He was in tears. He was sobbing. They weren't there.

She was sitting right behind him, hidden by a large boulder, with the children clasped tightly to her. She'd placed a hand over the youngest girl's mouth. Margrete glanced at Egil. Finally, she couldn't stop herself. She went up to him and embraced him. He put his arms around her and the children.

'Why do we always lack courage?' she said.

What had she meant? He was about to ask. Egil Halsteinson ran back to the farm. She called after him. He wouldn't listen. He fetched his horse and rode as hard as he could to Reykholt.

*

Before the day took on its colour, Reykholt was wrapped in a veil of mist. The ground was heavy with dew. The clouds had slept over the farm during the night. The North Star had been wiped out. Now they sank towards human and animal warmth. Soon the sun would be up and the mist slowly rising, leaving only a few white wisps above the house tops. A barely visible, silver-grey vapour rose from the ground. After a while it reached the church spire and finally into the clouds and the rain's childhood. Next came dark smoke from a couple of the open hearths, forming pennants of ash. No one on the estate knew where the last of the autumn swallows came from. All that they could see was that they flew to and fro over the circular pool. The small amount of green that was visible wasn't the dazzling green of summer but a green on the verge of darkness, in which one glimpses the earth beneath. In a few places in the barren landscape, steam was rising from the ground. The smell was sulphurous. The wind picked up. A door began to slam. The wind brought with it the remnants of words. It wasn't easy to tell if they came from earlier times or were shards of statements yet to be made.

'The likes of the brutality we've witnessed here in Iceland over the past few years couldn't be matched, not here nor anywhere else. Human beings must have learnt by now,' said the oldest woman standing at Snorre's feet that autumn day in 1241.

As she stared at Snorre's disfigured body, there came the sound of a voice she'd never heard before:

'Human beings have said what they had to say. Now they ought to rest. But they won't. They'll behave as if they're at the dawning of some great age, even though they're living in the last one. No matter what they do with and to one another, they never learn. Human beings always think their own time is the worst, and that things can't deteriorate further. They're living in the age of innocence. Men die, just as fire dies, without trace. The myths and golden illusions lie in the ashes. They have no history other than the fire.'

'But isn't there any hope?' the old woman wailed.

She drew breath before adding, as she was wont to do whenever she looked at a dead face: 'What was the point of *his* being born at all?'

In the grey light of dawn, a lone, exhausted horseman came riding up. He could barely stay on his mount. After he passed through the gate, he dropped his reins. The horse trotted calmly into the yard where Gissur and his men were making ready to leave after a couple of hours' sleep. The rider's eyes looked vacant. He dropped the reins again. He made no attempt to grasp them. His hands fumbled for the saddle. Finally, his right hand managed to grip the pommel. He was close to falling off his horse. The men couldn't tell if he was wounded. He was carrying a sword, a bow and arrows. None of the men knew him. Was he ill? His horse stopped in front of Gissur. The rider was unable to hold the top half of his body steady. It swayed from side to side. His head drooped forward.

Gissur wondered if the man was even able to see him. Two men ran up and helped him off his horse. Gissur and the man stood eyeing one another. He didn't even question why all these armed men were present. He'd obviously ridden the whole night. His face was tearstained. He scrutinized the men in front of him for a long time. Then he turned to Gissur and asked where Snorre Sturlason was. Gissur asked him to state his errand. There were long pauses between his words.

'What do you want with Snorre?' Gissur asked.

'I've come here to kill him,' Egil said.

Kyrre walked up to Egil and whispered a few words in his ear. Egil asked for something to drink.

AFTERWORD

I

The Little Horse is a novel about Snorre Sturlason and his last five days.

Snorre, the great Icelandic skald and statesman, realizes that he does not understand his own son; and he has sufficient insight to admit that he does not quite understand himself either. The countries of Iceland and Norway, their kings and rulers, however, *that* is something he understands.

This gifted author and historian was killed on the farmstead of Reykholt in Iceland, on 23 September 1241. It was pride that killed him. More than twenty years earlier, he had received gifts and titles from King Håkon of Norway in exchange for his promise to persuade Iceland's great men to submit their country to the Norwegian crown. Snorre believed that, due to his knowledge of the leadership in Iceland and Norway, he did not need to fear for his life in the autumn of 1241.

Our belief that we are able to understand our own, or future, society has not weakened with the years. Quite the contrary. A large number of journalists and researchers make a living that way—not to mention the politicians. If any man in the history of the world was capable of understanding his own society, it was Snorre. Born into the country's powerful elite in 1178, Snorre belonged to one of the eight families who owned the greater part of Iceland. At the age of three, he was sent to the mightiest man in Iceland, Jon Loptsson. His foster father was not only among the richest in the country but also the most learned. The chieftain court, Oddi, over which Loptsson ruled, was the only academy in North Europe at the time, an academy considerably influenced by the University of Paris. The philosophers of Antiquity, Greek, Latin and other languages, as well as geography, history, literary theory and theological disciplines, were all part of the curriculum. As were astronomy, lexical works on animals and countless written reports on various rulers in Europe. Snorre thus grew into an exceptional man of letters in the European sense. In his youth, and to an even larger extent as an adult, he had contact with cities like Constantinople, London and Rome. In 1206, he moved to Reykholt after marrying into wealth. He further augmented his financial power and was later elected lawspeaker, for a number of years, in the Althing, the oldest parliament in Europe. In reality, he was the chosen state leader of the island far out in the North Atlantic, armed with a unique insight into the country's various family networks.

In Iceland, Snorre is primarily recognized for *Edda*, a manual on the art of poetry, and for his survey of Norse mythology. In Norway, he is best known for *Heimskringla*, also called the *Sagas of the Norse Kings*, which most importantly deals with St Olav, the king who converted from a barbaric Viking to a fanatic Christian. The Icelandic skald also describes the history of the Norwegian kings up to the year 1177. In the young Norwegian state, Snorre's *Heimskringla* has been read, alongside the Bible, as scripture and been of vital importance to the formation of our national identity. As the *Heimskringla* was written on the instructions of the King of Norway, Snorre was given a unique opportunity to obtain insight into Norwegian and Swedish affairs.

Heimskringla is not only of literary importance, as Argentinian author Jorge Luis Borges, among many others, has pointed out. It is also impressive as a historical work. Great historians have compared *Heimskringla* with equivalent European works written in the Middle Ages, and Snorre has fared favourably in the comparison. In spite of all of Snorre's qualifications, however, he was unable to comprehend that ignoring King Håkon's prohibition to leave Norway and return to Iceland in 1239 was equal to meeting death. The same skald believed, to the end, that his achievements as author, orator and ruler, as well as the ability of his son, Orækja, to summon able-bodied men to defend the interest of the family, would save him from harm.

Before dawn on 23 September 1241, Snorre encountered his murderers, face to face. Then, at last, he understood that his common sense had not sufficed. There is no reason to reproach him for that. It is part of human nature, and we, who happen to live now—we have not learnt any better. Does it sound depressing? As soon as an optimist sees a light that does not exist, a pessimist comes along and blows it out.

II

In my historical novels, I have endeavoured to collect empirical material about the principal characters. I have read books and acquainted myself with the subject matter, written by my historical characters or by others, and I have travelled in their paths. Nevertheless, these novels cannot be considered biographies. Not even the cleverest biographer in the world can reconstruct a human life, nor can any of us fully understand a single individual.

Instead of using psychiatry, which considers it possible to classify people through diagnoses, I have chosen the form of the novel. I think it is the most suitable instrument for letting people know my intention, which is to *approach* the principal characters. It is I who have chosen to follow Snorre during his last five days, and it is I who attach importance to his relations, to his mistress, Margrete, and to his son. It is a subjective choice. I do not pretend to disclose everything about Snorre. Rather, it is the characters behind the ideologies that I wish to penetrate, the dailiness of their lives as well as the complexities of their psyches. My theory is that peoples' hearts and minds, across borders and through time, are surprisingly similar. We already know a great deal about the historical characters in my novel; we also have some knowledge about how they were regarded in their time. When I am writing about historical characters, I don't have the same freedom as when I'm writing pure fiction, where everything is created in my mind. But this is deliberate. By choosing a historical approach, I'd like to believe that I become more humble in my attempts to describe the principal characters. The historical novel, in my opinion, is very well suited to this task. Fact and fiction, elements of the short story and aphorisms all fit into the broad framework of a novel. The freedom to carry on when there are no more facts to refer to, as well as the literary approach, appeals to me. Through this work, and though my engagement with human rights issues while working on these novels, I have asked myself: When reason is absent to such an extent, is it not then the best solution to sit down and do what one can to not give in to despair? Some

have a dog or a cat they can talk to. Snorre had his little
horse. Most people have no one to talk to, and nothing to
believe in. For me, it is more odious not to engage in the
fate of the individual, concerning the right of man, than to
do so. Not that I am particularly noble but, as long as I
have received thorough knowledge of the case, it is difficult
to look the other way.

Furthermore, my experience with fellow beings in the
less peaceful parts of the world has shown me more of
their inner selves than I would otherwise have seen. In all
four of my historical novels, civil wars form the background.
That is hardly a coincidence.

Thorvald Steen
Oslo, 15 October 2013

(*Translated by Nora Skaug*)

REFERENCES

BAGGE, Sverre. *Society and Politics in Snorri Sturluson's Heim-skringla*. Berkeley: University of California Press, 2009.

ENCYCLOPÆDIA BRITANNICA ONLINE, s. v. 'Snorri Sturluson'. Available at: http://www.britannica.com/EBchecked/topic/550523/Snorri-Sturluson (last accessed on 4 August 2014).

JOHANNESSON, Jon, Magnus Finnbogason and Kristjan Eldjarn (eds). *Sturlunga Saga*. Reykjavik: Sturlunguutgafan, 1946.

JØRGENSEN, Jon Gunnar (ed.). *Snorres Edda i europeisk og islandsk kultur* [Snorre's Edda in European and Icelandic Culture]. Reykholt: Snorrastofa, 2009.

KRISTJÁNSSON, J. *Life and Works of Snorri Sturlasson*. Reykholt: Snorrastofa, 2013.

MONSEN, Erling. 'Introduction' in Snorri Sturluson, *Heim-skringla, Or The Lives of the Norse Kings* (Erling Monsen ed.).

Mineola, NY: Dover Publications, 1990, pp. *vii–xxviii*.

SIGURDSSON, Jon Vidar. *Chieftains and Power in the Icelandic Commonwealth*. Odense: Odense University Press, 1999.

WHALEY, Diana. *Heimskringla, an Introduction*. London: Viking Society for Northern Research, University College, 1991.

WITTMAN, Pius. 'Snorri Sturluson' in The Catholic Encyclopedia. VOL. 14. New York: Robert Appleton Company, 1912.